PERPETUALLY SINGLE GAL

H.E. Rae

Copyright: Elisa-Marie McRae
Vancouver, BC, Canada
October 2011
ISBN-978-1-105-17369-1

Chapter 1

Shanny is... attending Brian and Ryan's wedding.

Okay. So, maybe I should explain off the bat, Ryan is a girl. She's my girl friend. I mean my friend who's a girl. And when I say my friend who is a girl that is what I mean- she's not one of my friends who is a girl, she's my only friend who's a girl.

And now she's married to Brian. So I guess I'll have to start over and look for another gal pal, someone who also has two X chromosomes and understands that urgent, primal need for chocolate every twenty-eight days. (Who am I kidding? I need chocolate every twenty-eight minutes.)

Speaking of chocolate, this cake is seriously lacking. I can't believe they paid good money for this. (What is good money, exactly? Is there bad money?)

If I seem scattered, like I'm rambling, it's because I am. When I'm left to my own thoughts, they tend to wander, but not at some leisurely lackadaisical pace. It's as if they are playing some supped up school yard game of red light/green light. A shrink once told me to wear a rubber band on my wrist and snap it whenever I felt as though my thoughts were getting "off task." Well, that's a great idea, isn't it? Only two problems: one, I have an adverse reaction to the slightest sensation of pain and two, a rubber band is not a classy accessory, particularly when one is wearing a burgundy bridesmaid dress. (The bridesmaid dress= modern torture device, clown suit for the perpetually single gal.)

This particular dress is not especially hideous; there are no frills, no over-size bows. What is making me feel monstrous is the matching choker I've been forced to wear, like some sort of dog sporting a collar. Who is my owner in this scenario? Ryan? Well she did buy my dress, she is feeding me (and 150 other guests), and she does keep petting my hair telling me I look "soooo pretty." (I could definitely picture her talking to a dog like this.) The other two bridesmaids, Ryan's sisters, Joe and Tyler, appear to be oblivious to the sad state of our collective appearance.

As I swallow my piece of Styrofoam, I am only too aware of the choker fulfilling its destiny- choking me. I try to cough nonchalantly and sip my punch.

The problem with wedding receptions for the single gal, as I see it, is this- when you are left alone on the sidelines because there are no cute single guys to dance with, you are desperate not to appear as though you were relegated to the bench. You want to seem empowered. You chose to stand alone off to the side because you are a modern woman who does not need a man, you are comfortable in your own skin, you are Beyoncé, just waiting to tell someone they should've "put a ring on it" with that sassy swagger. So, what do you? You try to look occupied. You can't sit off and text- that looks rude ("what, you've got somewhere more important to be?") You can't take off your shoes and rub your feet. And you definitely can't go and talk to the old married couples. ("It'll be your turn next, dear." "How old are you? Oh. Oh my. Well, have you tried that internet?")

So, what do you do? You eat. Or you drink. And since I'm not one for alcohol, I eat. I eat cake. As though Mary Antoinette's alleged imperative was addressed solely to me, I devour that most disgusting of all wedding traditions, the three tiered, fondant-covered cake. (Why couldn't there have been a wedding chocolate fountain tradition? Or even a fruit tray tradition for crying out loud? Why did it have to be cake?)

I try to finish my last four or five bites of cake as I look around the room. The decorations are nice, pink and plastic, but nice. The servers are running around in their cummerbunds and bow ties clearing the dishes with half-eaten chicken Kiev or prime rib. Ryan is saying farewell to yet another old couple who interrupts her and Brian as they try to dance to

"Celebration." Brian pretends to smile at the old people while he desperately wants to get back to his robot moves competition with his best man, Sam.

Sam is a character. With his name, how could you blame him? Sam Samson Haire. That's his name. I'm not kidding. That's his actual name. But don't ask him what his parents were thinking when they named him that, he gets offended. Believe me, he doesn't like it. I found that out on our first and only date. I also found out that his car was "in the shop," he doesn't know how to bowl "without his own ball," and he has no problem letting a girl pay for the date because he "forgot his wallet." I think what I really learned on that date was that Ryan and I aren't as good of friends as I had thought. Could she really have believed he and I would hit it off? I'm not usually one to judge a guy for being bald or unemployed or socially awkward. But Sam Samson Haire is the holy trinity and I am not a devotee.

It could have been that Ryan just thought I was lonely or desperate (such a great suspicion- to think you send out those vibes) or it could have been that Sam had asked her to set us up. (On our first meeting he did compare me to a vase full of wild flowers.) Or it may be that I am right and that Ryan and I don't really know each other as well as either of us believes. I would venture to say that I know her better than she knows me; watching a friend go through a rough break up with someone you are also good friends with tends to give you a giant plexi-glass bay window into their psyche, their soul, whatever. (This illuminates what is definitely one of the pros of being the perpetually single gal- you maintain a modicum of mystery which you choose to brand as personal dignity. Being observed in a long-term/serious relationship requires a person to abandon all personal dignity at the front door under the welcome mat. You have the benefit of avoiding all of that. You are sooo lucky.)

At this moment, Ryan is motioning for me to join them on the floor for the Chicken Dance. Thank the Cake Boss, I have this plate in my hands and a fork full of stale sentimentality in my mouth. I shake my head apologetically communicating the complex thought- "I would love to but I have this piece of cake in my mouth and it would be rude to dance and eat at the same time and I just can't stop eating this cake because it is sooo good." She gets the whole idea, I can tell, and turns back to her new husband, and the balding biblical non-bowler who is way too into this song. I turn away from them, towards the entrance so that I can allow my face any natural response it wants to make without anyone seeing me or correctly interpreting my expression as mockery. (I can't help it sometimes my eyebrows have to raise, my eyes have to roll.) But my expression changes quickly enough. My eyebrows are stopped in their tracks. I can't believe it. Coen showed up.

He sees me, drops his envelope in the wishing well/money receptacle, and makes his way over. Of course, he is looking good as usual.

"Nice suit, Conrad," I say, sounding less sincere than I'd like. But he knows I mean it.

He grins, "Thanks." He pauses confidently and takes a deep breath scanning the room like a shark looking for bait.

"I can't believe you had the nerve to show up."

"I was invited, wasn't I?"

"You know perfectly well what that invitation meant, and it wasn't 'please arrive at our reception half way through in an expensive suit with the intention of stealing someone's date.'"

"Of course, that's what it meant. Don't be stupid."

"Coen, did you even RSVP?"

"I didn't come for the dinner, did I?"

"I can't believe you. Ryan is going to tweak. And she's been surprisingly normal all day so far. Maybe because she thought you weren't coming."

"I repeat, Shanny, I was invited."

"I repeat, Conrad, that invitation was not an invitation."

He is clearly enjoying this. "So, what was it then?"

"You are obnoxious. Let me explain this for the last time and then maybe you could go home. That invitation was Ryan's way of telling you she is over you."

"If that's what it was, she really shouldn't have bothered sending me one. All it really did was prove she still thinks about me."

"Of course she does. You broke her heart, you jerk."

"Hey now-"

"I mean it. You being here just supports the whole jerk theory."

"You know it wasn't all me."

I do know that. "Why are you here, Coen?"

"Don't change the subject yet. Say it. You know it wasn't all me."

"Yeah. I know that."

"She was crazy. Say it."

"I'm not going to say that."

"But she was. You know it."

"Conrad-"

"You know it."

"I know she didn't handle everything the best way."

"Is that as good as I'm going to get from you?"

"Tonight it is. It's her wedding after all. I think we should be nice to her for this one night at least."

"Fine. I concede the point. *(Wow, he smells good.)* You look great by the way. No, I'm serious. The choker is very sexy- you look very Nicole Kidman in Moulin Rouge."

"Her character had Tuberculosis."

"Well just think how above average sexy you have to be then to make that attractive."

"I'd rather not."

"You do look nice, though. How's the cake?"

I feed him a piece of it off my fork and his face says it all- he will not be asking for another bite, let alone grabbing his own piece. (Which to be fair, he shouldn't even get because he did not RSVP, the cardinal sin of omission for any wedding guest.)

"Coen?!"

The unmistakable squeaky voice of Ryan's younger sister Joe makes my ears ring ever so slightly. We turn around slowly.

"Hey there," he says flashing his charming grin at her.

"It is you! I just can't believe you are here! Does Ryan know? Let's not tell her okay? Let's just go dance, right now!" She pulls him eagerly to the dance floor and Coen either lacks the will or the strength to resist.

I give up watching them fairly quickly and decide I don't want to stick around for the next act. I'm happy to miss the dramatic confrontation when Ryan sees Coen. It's been almost seven months since I've had to listen to all the nitty gritty details and pretend to choose sides; there is no way I'm going through that again. Conrad may have been a jerk to her but he wasn't wrong- Ryan went nuts in that "I'm going to be the girl who convinces this guy never to have another relationship" way.

      I put down my cake though there is one bite left- as though abandoning it is some demonstration of self-control. I head to the coat check room to get my purse and my green trench coat. (I freely admit I didn't think this through- green trench coat with burgundy bridesmaid dress = disaster.) The noise from the hall fades away as I open the big double doors and head out into the early-ish night air.

      Is there anything more liberating than a huge inhale of fresh night air? (Okay, maybe a pair of Lulu Lemon sweat pants after a big lunch.) I try to walk over the cobblestone parking lot in my heels. Normally I am a rock star in these shoes but these bumpy stones make it impossible for anyone to look graceful. (Why did they install these anyway? They're not naturally occurring- did they really think the parking lot needed an old-timey atmosphere? Doesn't the presence of Dodge minivans and Toyota hatchbacks negate that detail?) These are the things I think about as I start my car and drive home.

These are the things I try to keep thinking about as I get cleaned up and into my pajamas. These are the things I try to think about so that the things that will make me feel lonely and unimportant can't keep me awake tonight.

Just as I'm about to fall asleep, my phone buzzes with that annoying text message alert sound that I haven't figured out how to change.

It's Coen- *I shouldn't have gone. Can you say awkward?*

The six-teen-year-old in me wants to text back, *Can you say Karma?* But instead I try to be mature about it. I type, *Call you in the morning* and I turn my phone off and fall asleep.

Chapter 2

Shanny is… procrastinating.

I definitely am procrastinating. Writing on Facebook that I am procrastinating is just another way of continuing procrastinating. Procrastinating. Procrastinating.

What am I procrastinating from? Well, so many things really. Cleaning, working out, looking for a new job. There it is- the clincher. My need for a new job. Can I really say it's a need? Maybe. I mean I make enough to get along at my current job. People are nice enough at Safeway. I just feel so stupid all the time- like how hard is it to remember the codes for seedless red grapes or for green chili peppers! It's really pretty hard actually. Joe would say it's sooo hard; but she quit the day after I got her the job so her opinion isn't really sooo reliable.

What drives me crazy is that I'm pretty sure I can do so many things. Lots of cool things. Just none of them will earn me any money. I think about becoming a professional mediator. Not a hostage negotiator or anything that intense but one of those corporate types who solve conflicts in the work place. The problem is I have no idea how you get trained for a job like that. (If it involves law school, I'll just have to forget it. There is no way I want to be a lawyer. I want to solve arguments, not generate them for a living.)

Other things I consider becoming but abandon almost immediately: a nanny, a film editor, a loan manager at a bank, a 911 call operator, or a florist. Being a florist is appealing to me. I love flowers- they make people happy, they smell good, they're pretty. What more could you want? Now that I think about it, maybe I shouldn't abandon this idea so quickly. I could take a class, maybe I could apprentice for someone. There are tons of flower shops down on Main; at least one of them must be willing to exploit my offer of free labor. I'll start calling later today.

Then I remember- the grocery store has a floral department and I have worked in it. Once. For one day. It was not such a good experience. But maybe it would be different in a floral shop, one with character. Maybe I could have a floral shoppe. You know, with the old-timey spelling? That has a charm to it, I think.

I consider running this idea by Coen but I'm pretty sure I can guess what he'd say. Likely I would get bored of it in a month. Probably I would give people deals for special occasions, refusing to profit off a birth, or a wedding, or (heaven forbid) a funeral. (And if you're not going to profit off those days what's left? Valentine's Day? Mother's Day? Two profitable days a year will not support a business.) I will spend all my pay buying flowers and bringing the nearly dead ones home so that they don't feel abandoned. He'll laugh at me for that. Also, Coen will tell me I'm meant for something better, whatever that means. I can't stand all the vague positive reinforcement.

I remember I told Coen I'd call him this morning. At last! A legitimate commitment that supports my procrastination agenda. It's not even the legitimacy of the commitment that makes me feel good. It's the wicked anticipation of whatever story he has in store for me. Coen has an eye for details and a mouth to share them but the best thing about his stories is that you can always believe them. He is not one to exaggerate.

That's why it was so hard for me to be there for Ryan when the bottom fell out; she would go on and on and on about Coen, about this and that but I could never believe what she would tell me. Her emotional reactions clouded her judgment and her memory. And she always thought I was some kind of traitor. I couldn't help not believing her; she just went, well, crazy. Coen isn't the kind of guy who goes in for long relationships in the first place and for her to pressure him the way she did after dating for two months- it was just nuts. (My inability to be empathetic wasn't helped by the fact that I could not relate to what was happening in any way, even though Ryan wouldn't have understood. She wouldn't have seen my status as the PSG as a disadvantage, as something that kept me from being on Team Ryan.)

When Coen told me about what happened between them, it made perfect sense. It was all clear and simple. Ryan wanted too much from him, too fast and he only wanted to test out the idea of them as a couple. Really, she couldn't fault him for that- he was honestly upfront about it all along. He's had enough girlfriends that for her to think she could tame him (isn't that a stupid term) was just crazy.

These are the things I think about as I dial his number.

"Morning, TB," he says.

"TB? That better not stand for Tuberculosis."

"No, no. It stands for either The Bridesmaid or The Bailer. Both are fitting after last night."

"I'm sorry, but I am not going to apologize. I didn't want to be there to witness the car wreck feature of the evening. But I am willing to listen to the gory details."

"Are you sure? They are pretty gory."

"Hit me."

"Well, after Joe dragged me on to the dance floor-"

"Completely against your will of course-"

"Will you let me finish?"

"Of course. Sorry." I can just picture the grimace on his face.

"So, Joe and I are dancing to an old Roxette song and-

"Wait. Wait. Wait. What Roxette song?"

"It Must Have Been Love."

"You're kidding me."

"No."

"Who plays that at a wedding? 'It must have been love, but it's over now.' That is not an apt lyric for the celebration of love newly unified."

"I know."

"Ridiculous."

"I know. Shanny- let me get back to the story, will you?" I stay quiet to show my willingness to listen. "Thank you. So, we're dancing, when Sam, your boyfriend, taps on Joe's shoulder to cut in. Joe shoves him away, honestly, shoved him away and tells him in that loud, screechy voice, 'No I won't dance with you now! I'm dancing with Coen!' Of course at that point Sam heads over to alert Brian to my presence but it's unnecessary since everyone heard Joe's yelling."

"Oh boy."

"It gets better. Brian storms up to me and demands to see my invitation, as though it's some sort of required ID to be in the room. I told him I didn't bring it. 'You mean you never got one,' he said. 'No,' I said, 'I mean I didn't bring it.' He won't let up. 'Then how'd you know how to get here?' he asks. And I'm about to tell him I've been to stupid weddings at this stupid golf course a dozen times in my life and I don't need directions from some lame invitation, but Ryan interrupts.

She grabs Brian's hands. And she looks deep into his eyes, and she says, 'It doesn't matter Bri. It doesn't matter. He doesn't mean anything to me anymore. He can't touch us. He can't come between this' At this point she puts her hand on his chest. Brian looks at me and then back at Ryan. He nods and kisses her way too intensely."

I know at this point he can picture the look on my face.

"I'm serious. Shanny, you should have seen it. They were barely even a foot away from me and Joe looked at me the whole time like it must be killing me to see this. Joe puts her hand on my shoulder and as the happy couple walks away, Ryan turns back to me and says, 'Sorry Conrad, you weren't the one. Sorry.'"

Conrad stops talking.

I wait.

I wait a little more.

I cannot wait anymore.

"Can I talk now?"

"Yes."

"Ho-ly. I can't believe it. She really did go crazy. And then did you just stay there? What did you do?"

"What could I do? I had a drink and I left."

"That's it?"

"That's it. Sorry, Shanny, if that's not awkward enough for you. It was more than awkward for me."

"You could have at least fished your card out of the wishing well."

"Wouldn't have been worth it. I only gave them 20 bucks in an envelope. I didn't even write in the card."

"Classy."

"I try."

"So, are we going to get together tonight?"

"Can't. Have a date."

"Oh. K."

"You don't want to ask who with?"

"Well, I'm assuming it's no one you met at the wedding, unless the choker thing really did catch your eye and you want to see if Joe is the mini version of Ryan."

"Definitely not."

I know he wants me to ask. He doesn't want to just tell me, he wants me to ask. "So, who's the big date with?"

"Val from work."

Oh. It's one of Coen's work girls. Can I admit that when I'm around them I feel like a twelve year old who doesn't quite know how to pick out a lipstick or tweeze my brows or fill out a shirt? They're all so put together and most of them are nice too, which is just unforgivable. (It means that hating them is entirely my own problem. I hate that!)

I haven't met Val but I'm sure she must be one of the sales reps. Coen works for a pharmaceutical company. He does something involved in arranging the overseas marketing campaigns (I honestly try not to listen too much; I worry it will force me to end our friendship. Some things are just unethical to an extreme. And I don't really have enough friends to sacrifice him for my middling ethics.)

Coen is forever dating the sales reps from his company. It's like the girls are factory models and he just keeps upgrading to the latest model until he finds a flaw or gets bored. (I honestly try not to ask too much about this either. Suffice it to say, I think it sucks.) I know he expects me to say something here.

"Well, I'm sure you'll have a great time."

"Hope so. You have any plans?"

"Didn't I just ask if you wanted to get together?"

"Sure, but I thought maybe you wanted an excuse to get out of something. There aren't any more wedding events?"

"No. The wedding is done and so am I. Besides, I doubt Ryan will want to talk to me very much after she finds out I know about last night or realizes that I ditched out without saying goodbye. Anyway, I think maybe I'll go for a walk tonight, maybe go to the park and try to find somewhere to bury that choker."

"You can't bury it! You have to keep it and wear it to your own wedding. It can be your something old."

"Well it will be old by the time I need it for that."

"No prospects?" Like he doesn't know. He knows it all.

"I'll never tell." I really won't.

We exchange the niceties of good byes and hang up. I really won't tell him. Sometimes I think there's nothing to tell but it's like I can't be sure. And if there's anything I like less than being unsure, it's being exposed.

Chapter 3

Shanny is ... home for Sunday dinner.

Mmmmm. The smells of my mom's kitchen on a Sunday afternoon. They're cyclical. I can tell how far we are into the month based on these smells. Lemon means it's the first Sunday of the month and we're having lemon chicken and lemon rice, probably with carrots. Roast means it's Sunday number two and we're having, predictably enough, roast- and potatoes. The third Sunday of the month? That's when things get interesting; the house fills with the smell of fresh basil and dried oregano- it's pasta night. The fourth Sunday is Mom's attempt to convert us all to vegetarianism by cooking Indian food so jammed full of spices and yogurty goodness that we shouldn't miss the meat.

On a special month, the kind that has a fifth Sunday, Mom makes soup, usually cheese and broccoli soup. The soup used to vary and be adventurous at one time I'm sure but Gavin, the youngest of us children, likes predictability. Predictably, the youngest got his way and soup day became broccoli and cheese soup day. (Not that I'm complaining too much- who doesn't like broccoli and cheese soup?)

Today happens to be pasta day, which is fine with me. The preparation is pretty simple and mom rarely needs any assistance. On pasta day usually all I'm asked to do is take the bread to the table or fill the glasses with water and two ice cubes each.

I notice that the table is set for only five people. What is happening here?

"Who's not coming for dinner, Mom?" I ask nonchalantly.

"Everyone's coming."

Right. Let's try this again. "I'm only seeing five place settings. Obviously someone is not coming."

"What?" she asks as she comes into the dining room, looking annoyed that I've interrupted her flow.

"Five settings?"

"Oh. Oh yeah. Right," she says and hurries back into the kitchen, to check on her sauce I presume.

My mother's not the most talkative person, but she's not usually this tight-lipped. I consider following her, pursuing my line of questions like a dogged paparazzi reporter, but instead the doorbell rings. (Doorbells are an excellent distraction.)

"I'll get it!" I call to her as I head to the door.

It's Liam. He's by himself.

"Hey Shanny," he says. "So, you survived the reception?"

I grimace. "That would be the right word."

Liam takes his time taking off his shoes. I've never known anyone else to be so careful about his laces. When we were kids and he tried to teach me to tie my shoes, he was so insistent that both ends had to be the exact same length and that I always had to double knot. I honestly think my refusal to have perfectly symmetrical bunny ears has led to some distance in our relationship.

"Too bad you couldn't make it," I say sincerely. Liam introduced Ryan and me. She was one of his first clients; I think she bought a two bedroom condo from him. They had a friendly relationship and he wound up inviting her to a party at his house, where he insisted that I give her a tour. (I think he's always thought it was strange that I have had so few girl friends. Maybe as my older brother he thought he should step in and save the day; I've certainly never needed any other kind of saving from him.)

"Well, Kim wasn't feeling well last night, and I couldn't leave her in the new house alone."

I raise my eyebrows as a question.

He explains, "She thinks it's haunted. It makes weird noises. It scares her. Really scares her."

From his tone, I'm not sure how he feels about this. I can tell he thinks it's a bit ridiculous but he is also defensive- he always has been about Kim. He may not be quite as amused as I am. I remember first meeting Kim and thinking that Liam was dating her on a bet. Honestly. (I know that sounds bad. But being so judgey is another part of the PSG's make-up. It's an instinct to look at someone who seems to be a piano with a few keys missing, and wonder how on Earth they have someone to love them and you don't. The more oddities you observe in this person blessed to be a couple with someone, the more you notice lacking in yourself, the more you try to comfort yourself by thinking, "at least I know how to pronounce prosciutto" and "at least I have two eyebrows" and "I'm just glad I understand the concept of sarcasm.")

Over time, I have realized that I was unfair to Kim, especially when I learned that she was an immigrant to this country and English was her third language. In spite of, or maybe because of that, we still aren't really close.

I am curious, though. "So, she couldn't be alone on Friday night but she's okay this afternoon?"

"No, she doesn't want to stay at home by herself. She would have come but her parents needed her to come over and work in their garden. They're getting pretty old and they need her help."

I forgot- Kim is really good at gardening. Sooo good. She always has fancy plants growing in their house and none of them ever look like mine- like criminals serving out their life sentences, desperately wishing they could just be sent to the electric chair and get it all over with. (Maybe I should talk to her about the whole florist thing. I make a mental note of this but secretly acknowledge to myself that I likely won't ask her.)

I'm about to ask Liam another follow up question to continue the small talk, when Connor comes bursting through the door. Connor and his stupid high levels of energy. It just makes me sick. No, not sick so much. Guilty. He makes me feel guilty all the time, as though it was his purpose on Earth to be better than me and to ensure that I know it. But any time he starts talking to me about taking herbal supplements or my need to enter a Fun Run, I just remind myself that he is the same boy who used to try to convince me to go out to the backyard and smoke pot with him behind the rundown doghouse (not built for our dog- we never had pets) before mom came home.

How he went from being a burn out to being obsessed with burning calories is still a total mystery to me. I rarely mention it unless I feel provoked. (Should I admit that I feel provoked all the time?)

"Hey there Shanny," he says with a big smile as he kicks off his sandals. "How long will you be untying those things?" he asks Liam and pats him on the shoulders. Liam rolls his eyes. (I knew it must have been a family trait! My genetics, or my environment, are definitely to blame for my slightly rude facial expressions.)

"Very funny," Liam says. "Why don't we just ask Shanny how long she'll be working at Safeway?"

Hey! When did this become about me?

"No time," replies Connor. "Gavin will be through the door any moment now."

On cue, Gavin comes in. He kicks off his shoes and dumps his backpack on the ground in front of the staircase.

"Mom will want you to move that," Liam warns warily.

Gavin laughs at his naivety. "Mom won't even notice it's there."

Gavin is right. When Mom hears the door close, she hustles into the foyer, acknowledging only Gavin's presence. It's not that I'm jealous- I mean he is the baby and he has gone away for school. (Well sort of away- is an hour from home, away?) Sometimes, though, I think it would be nice for her to be so excited to see me or to make the fifth Sunday into leek and potato soup day, seeing as it is my favorite. Just once. That would be good enough. (I'm pretty sure it would be enough.)

After all the hoopla of a mother son reunion, the four of us kids head into the dining room to wait for Mom. We do not touch our plates, or our flatware, or our glasses, or anything on the table. (One simply does not do that until dinner is served! Or so my mother insists.)

Gavin fills us in on life at the university. He is too busy studying to have a life, too busy having a life to study- you know that same balancing act the rest of us juggled. He includes me in his generalization even though we are all constantly aware of my drop-out-ed-ness. (I can't help that I realized I didn't want a business degree when I was 30 credits away from my

MBA. But why would I put in the work, or the money, or the time, to finish something that means nothing to me? It took only one course on sustainability and social justice for the developing world and I realized I just couldn't do the MBA route anymore.)

Connor is in the middle of preaching to Gavin on the importance of maintaining a balanced lifestyle and making time for the gym, when Mom comes in with a heaping plate of fusilli, my favorite noodles. Lately, she buys the whole grain kind so that Connor won't scold her for feeding us with refined carbohydrates. I know I'd rather have to chew my food a little longer than listen to a repetitive sermon on our family Sabbath.

"Smells great, Mom," says Connor admiringly. "But seriously Gav, you've got to consider your blood pressure. You're in a stressful, competitive environment. That can wreak havoc on your health. Have you ever considered a yoga class?"

We all know perfectly well that Gavin has never and would never consider taking yoga.

"Actually, I went last week," he answers.

Liam's eyebrows narrow so close together he almost matches his absent wife's uni-brow. "Really?" (At least he shares my disbelief.)

"Yeah. It was okay," Gavin says and passes the bowl of piping hot noodles to Mom.

"How did you end up in a yoga school?" Liam asks.

"It's called a studio," Connor interjects.

"Whatever. Why were you there, Gav?"

Gavin piles a mound of pasta on his fork so that he can take a deliberate bite as soon as he answers. (No one else may notice this but, as someone who has the need to avoid pesky follow up questions and statements of pity, I recognize this classic tactic.) The fork nears his mouth as he answers, "Tash took me." In goes the fork.

Wide smiles spread across my family's faces.

"I knew it!" cries Connor, who forgets his manners and slaps the table. "I knew she was perfect for you."

"Working out together, that's a big deal," says Liam with his eyebrows now rose in an opposite direction.

"How nice, Gavin," says Mom as she sips smilingly from her water glass.

Gavin has a lot of food to chew, leaving a considerable gap, which Connor fills. "This is perfect, Gav. What are you guys doing this weekend? Megs and I are going to the free concert in the park after the Cops for Cancer Walkathon. Why don't you two come with us?"

Gavin has finally chewed his food and answers Connor. "We are coming with you. Meaghan invited us last night. I won't be able to come to the Walkathon though, too much studying to do. Tash and I are going to pick up dinner and bring it over to you guys and we'll eat during the concert."

(Wait for it. Connor's caveats are coming.)

"Make sure the food is from the organic market. Megs won't eat it otherwise. Nothing too heavy. We'll be tempted to eat too much after so much exercise and that is not a great idea. And don't worry about dessert. We don't eat dessert."

"I love dessert," I say.

Everyone ignores me. (I guess that's better than some sassy comment like 'obviously' or 'that's why you have to wear those pants, is it?')

I can't help myself. I go on, "Especially, chocolate."

"Shannon, what are you going on about?" My mother is easily frustrated.

"I just wanted to ask Gavin how it feels to be dating his brother's girlfriend's sister, that's all."

They all look at me quizzically.

"It's not a big deal, Shanny," say Gavin and Connor at the same time. (Oh brother, why don't we buy them matching condos and get it over with.)

"It's just about time Gav here gave someone a chance. He had to eventually realize there's more to life than his giant brain," continues Connor.

"Right. There's chocolate."

"Shannon! Really. I've no idea why you are so ridiculous some times." (See? I told you she is easily frustrated.)

Mom, Gavin, and Connor continue their discussion of weekend plans and Liam tries to save me from the tedium of listening to them by replacing it with the tedium of grilling me about job prospects. I think he just wants me to bring home a bigger paycheck so that I'll buy one of these new fancy condos he is developing. That may just be my cynical nature. (Can I have a cynical nature or is cynicism learned?)

I tell Liam about my florist plan and he suggests I talk to Kim. Then he suggests I talk to one of his clients, some old guy named Chance Barley, who does a lot of business with some of the more upscale florists in town. Liam plans to call me with Chance's info. I thank him, knowing I will most likely, like 99% likely, not call this guy. But hey, at least Liam cares enough to try.

He keeps trying, insisting that I must call this guy, as we all tidy up and head out the door. Liam promises to follow up with me at next Sunday's dinner and he says he'll ask Kim to bring me some plants to "practice" with.

I think sometimes that he feels like has needs to take care of me. He is the oldest. Dad died when he was ten and I was five so Liam has always been that responsible alpha-ish male. (Connor is a year younger than me and Gavin is three years younger than him.) We never had money troubles. For some reason I think Liam has always anticipated that, while Mom can take care of herself, I am incapable of such a feat. So long as he is nice about it, I don't really mind.

Too much. After all, what do I have to prove him wrong? My dingy apartment? My fab job at the Safeway? My almost, but not quite, paid off student loan that didn't result in a degree? Oh wait I know- my lack of prospects for the future and my status as the PSG of the family. At least I have a great collection of jackets. And I have plans. I do. I'm just not sure what they are yet.

Chapter 4

Shanny is... sooo tired. Also, I am planning on punching the next person who insists to me that the customer is always right.

Connor Hardy- That doesn't sound like a very positive attitude Shan. Maybe you need to try some herbal tea.

Muriel Hardy- Listen to your brother, you can't afford to lose your job.

Shanny Hardy- Can't I just rant without a family lecture? What is the point of Facebook if I can't?

Gavin Hardy likes this.

Chapter 5

Shanny Hardy is now friends with Ryan Cooper-Kokozka

My friendship with Coen is sometimes a mystery to me. Today, not so much. When I need to laugh, he is usually my own personal Conan O'Brien sans the red hair, albino skin, and Irish ancestry. (I'm the Irish one in our friendship. He's the dark handsome one.)

I have been nervous all morning. It's only Wednesday, but my wonderful brother Liam has already put his plans for my future into reality. He called Chance Barley (on my behalf) first thing Monday morning. Liam has told me that the conversation was fairly casual, that there is no pressure attached to this morning's meeting, but I have other theories. One is that Liam has given back the commission he made from Chance's latest real estate acquisition in exchange for my interview. (Is this an interview? No? What is it? I honestly don't know.) Another one is that Liam has explained to him that I am single, desirable, and looking for a May-December romance as well as employment.

I need to calm down. Now. Well, ASAP anyway. So, I call Coen.

"Talk to me TB," he says in his most officious voice.

"Knock it off with the TB!" I plead.

"Oh Shanny, get a sense of humor."

"I'll get one of those when it suits me. Today I need you to lend me yours."

"That's an odd thing to say. What's going on?"

"Liam got me a job interview with Chance Barley."

"With who?"

Why is he talking so loud?

"Chance Barley," I repeat, over-enunciating each syllable.
"Charles Barkley?"

"No! Chance Barley, the investor, not Charley Barkley, the basketball guy! Can't you hear?"

"I can hear you better now. Sorry. We were going through a tunnel."

"We? Who are you with? Why are you in a tunnel?"

"It's just me. I just like to speak in the plural."

"You're so weird."

"You love me."

Sometimes. It's undeniable.

"Where are you?"

"I'm on my way to work."

"Now? It's 10:30."

"Yeah, I thought I'd try to be on time today, you know, be a good team player."

"You are just so nuts some time. How you haven't been fired, is a mystery to me."

"I'll solve the mystery for you right now. Coen equals good pitch man equals brings in money for company equals job flexibility." The way he says 'flexibility' makes me want to pinch his arm. Hard. What a tool, what a confident tool.

"Well, congratulations to you, sir. We need to talk about something else before I get nervous about the fact that Shanny equals few skills equals low earning potential equals permanent Mcjob."

"How shall I distract you?"

"Any good stories lately?"

"Well, not so much. I could tell you about my dates over the last few days." Did he say dates? How did he have time to go on dates since last Saturday?

I have to ask, "Were these all with Val?"

"Yeah, they were."

I'm surprised.

"And they were good?" I ask, trying to sound completely cool.

"Yeah, they were." He sounds so happy. A thought crosses my mind.

"Are you coming from her place?"

"What? Shanny! What kind of question is that for you to ask?"

"Sorry. I didn't think you'd be so taken aback." Really, I didn't. I thought he'd just smile in slight shock and, maybe admit it, maybe not.

"You're just not usually so upfront."

"What does that mean?"

"Nothing bad." Sensing that I'm not buying it, he shares some news with me. "Things are going fast with Val but they're going good. She has enough sense to want her own space and she's only called me twice since Sunday. It's a good start for us."

Us? Us, already? I don't interrupt. I want him to continue.

"Speaking of a good start, Shanny, you calling is a great start to this day. I needed to ask you for a favor."

"Oh?"

"Can you feed Emperor for me? I'll be out of town for a week. I'm leaving Tomorrow."

"Of course. Not a problem." Whenever Coen goes out of town, I take care of Emperor, his mammoth beast of his dog, who happens to love me. Emperor is a Great Dane. (I know, I know. Who owns a Great Dane nowadays? And who can afford to feed one? Coen can and I pretend I can when I dog sit for him.) I just love walking through the door, hearing his deep bark, and then hurrying to avoid his huge body, which can easily knock me over. But whenever I'm in the house Emperor follows me around like a puppy in love, (like he's Emperor Napoleon and I'm Josephine.)

"Great. He's been missing you, Shan. It's been a while since you've been over."

"Yeah. Well, we've all been busy. You, me, Emperor- we've all been busy."

"You certainly have. And you'll be even busier once you get this job."

"Nope. No, back on to you please. I'm not ready to think about that yet."

"Sure. Why don't we talk about how much you're going to miss me while I'm in France?"

So, it's France this time? He's so lucky. Wait. Let me quote Ryan's sister- he's 'sooo lucky!'

"Why don't you tell me what you'll bring me back as a thank you gift?" Really, it's an unnecessary conversation- Coen is a great gift-giver. (Way better than anyone in my family. One year for my birthday, Mom got me a cookbook, Liam gave me a Safeway gift certificate, Connor got me a two month trial gym membership, Gavin got me a desktop calendar, and Coen gave me an emerald green pashmina he had picked out for me on a recent trip from Italy. Best gift? No contest.) My closet is salivating over what he may bring back from Paris. Ooh la la.

"I'll get you something nice. Don't even worry about it."

"I won't." There's a knock at the door. "I have enough to worry about."

"Is he there?"

I sigh. "Yes. This is going to be awful."

"Just tell him what's in your heart."

"What? Coen, you are not helpful."

"You'll be fine Shanny. Hey- I just thought of something."
"What?"

"You should put that bridesmaid choker on, for good luck."

"Good bye, Coen."

"Au revoir, Shanny."

We hang up. There's another knock at the door. After a quick glance in the mirror, I pull my bangs out of my face and open the door. Oh wow.

Oh wow.

I mean- wow.

He is so hot.

He's tall-ish, blonde-ish, and his jaw! I mean, his jaw!

Okay, Shanny, stop staring! Say something!

"Mr. Barley?" I ask and abruptly stick out my hand for an oh-so-professional hand shake, just the kind Liam has been forcing me to practice since I was a little girl

He takes my hand (firmly, but not too firmly) and smiling, shakes his head. "Oh- sorry, no. Mr. Barley's my uncle. He couldn't make it here this morning, a big meeting came up at the last minute, and he asked me to come in his place. He promised your brother after all, and my uncle takes his promises very seriously." It is taking all the concentration I have to listen to his words and not just stare at his mouth. (Here is another benefit of being a perpetually single gal- you experience no guilt over feasting on eye candy. Also, you experience no shame- as long as he can't tell he's being ogled.)

I have to tell him the truth right away, and just hope he finds it endearing. "I really hate to sound stupid, I even hate saying that I hate to sound stupid," I say, "but I'm not really sure what you're here to talk about. Am I being interviewed for something? Is there a position open in your company?"

"You don't know why I'm here?" he asks, his eyebrows raised. (His eyebrows! I think I'm in love.) I shake my head and smile apologetically. Oh no. He's going to think I'm an idiot.   Instead, he surprises me- he laughs. "Well, I guess we're stuck then. I'm not really sure why I'm here either. I was just told about this." He smiles at me as if we share a secret now. (I no longer think it- I am in love.)

So, I decide to pull out the greatest weapon in my arsenal. Ridiculous sarcasm. Someone please stop me. I just can't help myself. "You know, I've just remembered something," I say and snap my fingers. "My brother said Mr. Barley was coming by with a cheque for me." Oh no. What am I doing?

"A cheque?"

"Yes. For half a mil." Oh no. No. No. If he was still in the door way, I would just close the door, lock it, turn off the lights, and hide out in bed.

He pretends to check his pockets. "Right. The cheque for half a mil. Sorry, I left it in the car." Wait. Did he just-? He did. He keeps going, "It's just that I have to drop so many of them off that I forget sometimes. Please don't take it personally. Unfortunately, the cheque expired five minutes ago. So, too bad."

"That is too bad; I could really use the money."

"I could too," he says with a laugh. I accidentally raise my eyebrows at him, looking skeptical. "I mean it. My uncle is not the most generous man you'll ever meet."

"What do you mean? Actually, don't answer that. Forget I asked. It was nosy, none of my business."

"No worries. You'll have to excuse me, I've just realized I haven't told you my name. Hi. I'm Charlie."

He's kidding right? I forget to conceal the look on my face.

"What's the matter?" he asks.

I try to be tactful. "Your name is Charlie Barley? Your parents named you Charlie Barley?" (What's his middle name, "gnarly?")

He bursts out laughing (apparently this is a new joke.) "No. No, I'm not Charlie Barley. I'm Charlie Turcotte. Chance Barley is my mother's brother, my maternal uncle. Even my parents wouldn't do that to a kid. No one has ever asked me that before. Can you believe that? I can't believe that."

"I can't believe that either. It's not a giant leap or a clever insight."

This struck him as even funnier.

"It's really not," I say. He calms down. "I'm Shanny, by the way. Well, Shannon, but everyone calls me Shanny."

"Nice to meet you, Shanny," he says and extends his hand to me. A perfect shake this time, if I say so myself. "So, since neither of us know what is supposed to happen here, why don't we arrange for another time to meet, a time when we have some idea about what's going on?"

This sounds promising but I don't want to appear too eager. "That would be great," I say in a pleased and confident way.

"Great. And this time, my uncle will come and I won't waste your time."

Oh.

Come on, Shanny, recover!

I smile and nod. "Sounds good."

"Bye, Shanny. It was nice to meet you."

Well this is a most abrupt good bye after such a promising beginning. I still smile. "Bye Charlie. Nice to meet you, too."

As he leaves, I close the door and I can hear him chuckling to himself down the hallway. It sounds like he's repeating 'Charlie Barley!' followed by a chorus of giggles. I guess I'm funnier than I thought. He thought I was funny. Maybe that means something. Maybe not. I half smile, deciding to think it does mean something.

I also decide I like this day. I begin to imagine a future, my future career. The vision involves this: I wake up early in the morning to the sound of my husband humming in the shower (at this point in our marriage I still think it's cute) and I dramatically cast aside the curtains in our room to let in the sun. (Of course it's sunny in my fantasy.) The view outside is quite lovely. I head downstairs and eat my super-powered, ultra healthy breakfast of Greek yogurt, muesli, and berries. It gets me geared up for a high-powered day of decision-making and motivational leadership.

Then, Charlie comes down stairs. He kisses me on the shoulder and smells like his new shaving cream, like jojoba and lemongrass (I bought it for him, of course, even though I have no idea what jojoba is.) While he makes his protein smoothie and eats his toast, I have my shower, do my hair, and get dressed in my black and grey power suit. Charlie and I drive to work together, singing along to the radio as we drive in our hybrid. The day passes quickly and then we are glad to be home, preparing a dinner for two. Bliss. (Is it bad that in my career fantasy I don't even know what my career is?)

Of course this is all ridiculous speculation, but what if? What if? My fantasizing is interrupted by my phone buzzing. The familiar grating sound of someone butting in on my reveries via cell tower.

It's a message from Coen- Still in the interview? Show some skin!

Does he really think I would check my cell phone during an interview? No, he knows I wouldn't. He's just being himself- a confident, successful tool.

I text back- I showed him enough. He left almost immediately.

I think about calling him to tell him about Charlie but what would be the point? This is where I really wish I had a girl friend, someone to call and gush about meeting a new guy, even when there is no possibility of it going anywhere, it's still fun to fantasize and share your ridiculous dreams with a female friend. (At least I imagine it must be.)

Another text- Seriously, Shanny, I'm sure you did great.

Sometimes he's really very sweet.

-Have a great trip Coen. Don't worry about Emperor. He will be well taken care of.

-I'm sure. Bon chance, mon amie!

-Bon chance.

Chapter 6

Shanny is... regretting poor life choices and waiting... waiting... waiting...

Sometimes I question my need to put details about my life on Facebook. But not enough to stop doing it...

Oh man. The rain just won't stop. It's as though the clouds decided to have some sort of fundraising marathon- a deluge-a-thon. What they're raising money for, I have no idea. Maybe climate change?

It's been three days and neither Charlie non-Barley nor Chance Barley has called to set up that next meeting. Good thing I have my delusions to keep me going. Well, I don't know that I have delusions but I definitely have good dreams lately. (Last night Charlie and I were having a baby. The best part was that he kept giving me the most amazing back massages. And he still smelled like jojoba. By the way, when did jojoba become popular? What is it?)

At this moment it is I giving someone a back rub, not me getting the magic fingers. The lucky recipient? Emperor, of course. And he could not be more thankful.

How can anyone not love dogs? They give you so much love back. (I can understand not owning one- I don't own one- but not loving them is beyond me.) Any time I stop scratching his back he looks at me with the most promising yet pathetic face I've ever seen and I can't help but recommit myself to alleviate all his itches and find the perfect spot. You know, the one which, when you hit, the dog's back leg kicks and shakes like a jackhammer? I have to say I love that. It's a source of pride that I can always find Emperor's spot. Maybe that's why he loves me so much. (Do guys have a spot? I mean, emotionally? I definitely need to figure that out.)

Conrad's apartment is surprisingly manly. Not that he isn't manly- he just doesn't seem like the sports paraphernalia type when you first meet him. (But he does have autographs and pictures of hockey teams in the house.) His house is really nice but not fussy, though there are some rooms that I feel weird about going into when he's not home, like his den where he does his work. It's pretty baller, I have to say. The furniture is sweet, especially his fancy desk chair. It seems like the kind of chair a super villain would park himself in while dictating his latest evil plan to his cronies or henchmen. It's pathetic, I freely admit, butt this chair is so intimidating to me that I can't go on the computer for fear of sitting in it.

The room I live in whenever I spend time at Coen's house is the media room. This room is like Mecca to me. The only thing that would make it any better would be if there was some sort of dispenser to supply me with constant chocolate treats. (I will never admit that I have brought bags of different candies and hidden them among his DVD's and books. I am so dedicated to healthy eating that I did not hide a bag of Cadbury Éclairs in his den/office and I am not eating two of them right now.)

He has a pretty good DVD collection, though he owns more movies than he's ever watched, I'm sure. In a way, it's kind of my fault. I'm always telling Coen about classic movies or critically acclaimed new films that we have to see. He buys them, promising that we're going to watch them together. I think we've watched twenty, maybe twenty-five, movies over the past three years. Not a terrible record, but not all that great either. The best one we've seen in a while happens to still be in the DVD player. "Rushmore" was great.

Tonight, though, I'm not in the mood for cinema. Tonight I am performing the perpetually single gal's most feeble ritual- a Friday night spent with TLC. (Can someone explain to me why it's The Learning Channel? Who do they think they're kidding? TLC actually stands for The Loser Club- who else but the perpetually single gal, the ultimate loser, would sit at home on a Friday night watching 'Say Yes to the Dress' or 'Ultimate Cakes' or any number of shows about little people and oversized families?)

I remember once forcing Conrad to watch Cake Boss. I thought he was going to permanently end our friendship half way through the episode. He apparently does not want to be a part of The Loser Club. (Identifying TLC as The Loser Club is not an insult, after all I am the one watching it on a Friday night by myself in my friend's house while he's in Paris with his probable new girlfriend and- oh I cannot go on. Back to something else.)

The wedding shows are of course what I am after tonight, my Friday night feels-bad-but-somehow-feels-good fiesta. I can say all the judgy things I'd like to say at real weddings to the idiots on the TV (idiots who I am honestly jealous of I admit.)

A young bride, anyone younger than me getting married I now classify as a young bride, is trying on a kind of skanky Panina Torney. (Really? Do you need cleavage, a high slit, and a see though midriff on your wedding day?) It is really not working for her but she says yes to the dress and the consultants are sooo excited.

Emperor is staring at me. I've been neglecting my role as backscratcher.

"I'm sorry buddy," I say and resume the actions. I zoned out, imagining which of the dresses I would choose which then leads me to the negative self-talk that reinforces my identity as the PSG. (And here I am without a rubber band to snap.)

Once the show ends, I turn off the TV and fill Emperor's bowl for tomorrow morning. I've got to get home pretty soon. (I cannot sleep here. No matter how many times Coen insists it's not weird, it is weird.) But I decide that Emperor is such a good dog that he needs a treat. I'm pretty sure Coen left the treats somewhere in a drawer in his kitchen. I am terrible at finding things. I assume the dog treats are not in the bottom cupboards, so I pull the knobs on all the upper drawers. I see cutlery, extra keys, a phone book, oven mitts (he owns oven mitts?), wooden spoons, a can opener, take out menus, and a ring box. Hang on. What?

I look closer- it's definitely a ring box. It says De Beers on it for Pete's sake. What is he doing with this? Oh man. I really want to look at this. Oh I really, really do. But I can't. This is beyond personal. I cannot look at this. Then why am I opening this box?

Oh my.

The ring takes my breath away.

I never thought I liked diamonds. Well, I was wrong. Big time wrong. I love them.

(I wish I could describe it but I have no idea what a carat is, what the shapes are called, etc.) As much as I am hypnotized by the ring, my mind wanders, no it doesn't wander, it takes off like a fighter jet. Why does Coen have this ring? Why on this green earth beneath my feet does Conrad Marks have a diamond ring in his house? Why is he keeping it in a drawer in his kitchen? What is going on?

And most importantly, who is this ring for?

Chapter 7

Shanny is… listening to Said the Whale on her iPod before she goes to work.

Work is okay today I have to say. I mean, things could always get a lot worse. A lot worse. (But they could be way better. Why don't I ever focus on things getting better instead of just not worse?)

It is pretty slow for a Wednesday night so I wind up not being needed at the till punching in numbers, asking customers if they had air miles or a club card or what have you. (It's actually somewhat surprising how many people apologize for not having a club card. Why would I care? Honestly. No skin off my nose if you don't want to be tracked through our system.) Anyway, so, instead of working the till as a number-punch jockey, I am assigned that most glamorous of grocery store monolith jobs- the bag boy (or girl in this case.)

It's actually not as bad as people might think (not that I know what people think.) People seem to be generally appreciative when you bag their groceries, making sure the eggs don't get crushed by the yogurt or that their bread doesn't get smooshed by the cans of soup and tomato sauce. (I love when you see people who are so proud of themselves for bringing their own bags. I'd probably be proud too if I had exerted my mental powers to save the planet one plastic bag at a time. What heroes! Maybe we should make them badges or pins to wear, humbly proclaiming their commitment to Mother Earth. We could make them out of their old plastic bags.)

Tonight is slow. The store is full of mostly moms pushing their half hopefully filled carts- varying combinations of produce and sugared cereals competing for dominance. Of course the real contest is at the table where the kids choose the winner. Spoiler alert: processed sugar knocks out the beans and fiber every time.

Hey- this is new! My attentions are diverted from my action-packed alimentary imaginings back to reality. This must be the oldest lady I've ever seen in real life. Her hair is literally blue. This detail is almost obscured by the plastic rain bonnet thing she is wearing on her head. I have to admit, her matching rain coat is pretty darn cute. She looks shrunken and that miniature state makes her movements appear surprisingly spry and intense.

She slams her oranges down on the scale, declaring, "These better be naval oranges." (Or else what grandma?)

Lucy, at the till, assures her with a sweet smile that they are. Lucy is a really nice person, for a fifteen-year old. (If she was older, the two of us would definitely be gal pals and I wouldn't need to feel so stranded among the XY's in my life.) I don't think I've ever heard her say one bad thing about anyone in this place, which is pretty impressive- there are tons of people who deserve to be talked about. (Oh that was mean, wasn't it?) But Lucy is not one of them.

After her first day, I was sure I liked her more than most of my other coworkers. She brought cookies in for her first full day of work. Who does that? And during her break, she taught Christophe how to fill in Sudoku puzzles (easy level of course.) No one I know has the patience to talk to Christophe for more than a few seconds. The guy mumbles excessively. This is why he works in the bakery, away from the customers, I think. Anyway, Lucy spent her entire break talking to him. She even laughed at (what I can only guess was) an incomprehensible joke about numbers, or the Japanese, or maybe about one of us.

When I asked her how she got so nice, she laughed at me. So, I tried a different question. I asked her what classes she was taking and what she was planning to study in post-secondary. Well, she wasn't sure what she wanted to do in the future but she was spending most of her spare time volunteering with the Special Olympics. Her younger sister bowled with them and Lucy was an assistant. (I have no doubt that Lucy's little sister would be able to trounce my monsieur amour with or without his own ball.)

It was impossible not to love Lucy- even for a do-gooder, she was perfectly likeable. (Plus I once saw her role her eyes at a customer who, due to a shortfall of cash, decided not to buy a head of broccoli and a sack of potatoes in order to afford a pack of cigarettes. She tried to deny it, but smiled the whole time. Yep, Lucy is likeable.) I always like being the bag boy to Lucy's teller.

Lucy punches in the code for naval oranges, 20311, I think, and tells the lady her total, "That comes to $8.95."

"That will be fine." She hands a ten dollar bill over to Lucy, who makes change, or rather the machine makes change, rather quickly. The old lady says, "I'll need help out with my bags."

Is she serious?

"Now please, young lady, if you would do your job," she says to me in an irritated tone.

She does mean it apparently.

"Do you want your bag of oranges bagged?" (You bag.)

"Of course, Dear. Paper please."

"We only have plastic." Am I really having this conversation?

"Oh. Oh, that's too bad. Well," she sighs, "I guess plastic will just have to do. Double bag it. Let's go."

With that command, I grab the bag and follow the lady out to the parking lot. (I am fighting the urge not to swing the bag around. Oh man. I imagine swinging them 'around the world' style and the oranges falling down on me. What would she say then? I'm not sure but I could reply, "Orange you at least glad they didn't fall on you?" Sooo clever.)

I am wondering what sort of car this old lady drives as we go farther and farther to the end of the parking lot. We're heading pretty far. There aren't many cars back here, only a Ford F-350 and a VW van. Probably neither of those belongs to her. I decide to ask.

"Excuse me ma'am, which is your car? Or where is your car?"

"Oh, I don't have a car."

What?

"I'm sorry?" I say trying my hardest to sound polite.

"Not all of us are rolling in piles of money young lady, I can't afford a car. I take a bus. You know the cost of a bus pass is really so reasonable now with senior citizens' discount. We're really so lucky that our mayor has fought for senior's rights in this day and age."

What is she going on about? Wait a minute. Is she going to ask me to take the bus? With her? What the-?

"My bus will be here in ten minutes," crazy bag lady tells me. "You can wait with me until then," she says magnanimously as she sits on the bench, taking up the entire bench with her tiny body and her giant old lady purse, full of mints and used tissues no doubt.

"Umm, ma'am? I am sorry but I can't wait out here with you. I have to get back inside."

"No you don't. It's not busy in there."

"Maybe not, but I can't wait out here for ten minutes. My manager would be upset."

"Upset that you are assisting an elderly woman? No, no he wouldn't."

"Ma'am, really, I have to go back to work." I hold the bag towards her.

"You are working," she says and pointedly puts her hands on her lap.

"Ma'am, please take your oranges. Or, here, why don't I put the oranges in your purse?" There must be room for them in that mammoth carpet bag of hers. I lean forward to put them in. She slaps my hand! Unbelievable! What is wrong with this lady? She's two bags short of a Louis Vuiton expo.

"Young woman! Show some respect!"

I have to get out of here. She won't move, won't let me put the oranges on the bench or in her purse. I do the only thing I can think to do. I put the bag on the ground, I turn, and I run.

What am I doing? I don't know, but I'm doing it fast. I hustle back towards the store entrance. I hear the old lady calling something to me. Did she really just say that? I didn't think nice old ladies knew the word, F-

Ow! The last thing I see is a middle finger. Everything goes black.

Chapter 8

Shanny is... ?

So, here is what happened, so far as eye witnesses have recounted the events:

1) I was not paying attention to the vehicles in the parking lot. (Obviously not, an old lady was giving me the middle finger salute.)

2) The driver of the VW van pulled out of his spot, way too fast, cutting off some kind of early 90's Civic.

3) The driver of said Civic swerved and accelerated at the same time.

4) The driver of said Civic then slammed on breaks upon seeing Shanny Hardy in the parking lot.

5) The driver of said Civic was not fast enough to respond.

6) Shanny Hardy was ploughed.

(Okay ploughed is not the right term.) Apparently, the Civic hit me and knocked me forward. The reason I don't remember any of this? Car hit me, I hit the ground, brain hit inside of skull which means concussion and black out for Shanny.

I can't remember anything except the crazy old bag lady. Did she will this to happen? I bet she sat there grinning, just hoping that another type of bag would be brought by for only my use. (Okay maybe that's too harsh- she probably didn't want me to die. Probably.)

So, now I am lying in this hospital bed, unable to partially remember the accident, but able to completely feel the effects. My chest is killing me (I have four broken ribs); my neck feels like there is a rod in it (no rod, but I will have a brace for a while); my arms are burning (they're scraped and raw, covered in bandages now); and my face feels swollen and hot (stitches, bruising, scrapes, and puffy lips- just what every girl wants- I'm like Angelina Jolie, if she had been run over by a train.)

I feel like an idiot. I mean it wasn't my fault. It could have been worse. But who gets hit by a car in the parking lot? Who gets knocked out in the parking lot at their work? At a Safeway?

Oh and even worse- in this hospital you have to pay for TV and I refuse to pay- it's a rip off. Normally, I would turn to my iPod for comfort but it's at work and I'm sure no one has time to go and get it for me.

Liam did have time over the last day and a half to stop by with a book, "Knight in Shining Armor: Discovering Your Lifelong Love" by P.B. Wilson. Apparently some of the ladies in his real estate office swear by the book and they've been encouraging him to buy it for me for a while now. Liam figured that since I would have so much time now in the hospital, this would be my perfect chance to read it. (It was nice not to have to smile when saying thank you- anyone can see how much pain I'm in. Yes. That's it. The pain. That's the only reason I'm not gleeful about receiving a book filled with relationship advice while I'm lying in a hospital bed- it's only the physical pain, that's all.)

Kim came with him and brought me a plant, a really beautiful green Paphiopedilum orchid. (When I couldn't pronounce it, Kim helped me out by telling me they could also be called Lady Slipper Orchids.) That was really nice of her. She even spent a few minutes telling me how to take care of the plant- filtered light, good drainage, good air circulation, etc. As she was explaining all this to me, I think it dawned on her how unlikely it was that someone stuck in a hospital bed for who-knows-how-long would take good care of it. She suggested that she would take it home and "raise" it (she really used the word raise, as though the plant was a child) until I was back on my feet. I nodded. What a perfect idea.

Connor came by this morning and promptly launched into a speech about the travesty of the lack of nutrition in hospital food. I had to remind him that I am not responsible for the hospital kitchen. He promised to bring me some herbal tea and some digestible alfalfa crackers later today. Megs, who came with him, smuggled me some chocolate. (The good stuff, Callebault.) I'm wondering at this point how often she hides this stuff from Connor. She was really good at getting it to me without his notice. (Connor always insists that they don't eat dessert. Well, maybe he doesn't. But Megs does. The girl knows her chocolate.)

I still haven't seen Gavin. I'm not expecting him to come. He is really busy with school; if his grades slip he may not get a scholarship next year. Mom stopped by this morning and she says she was here last night, but I wasn't awake. I didn't wake up for something like 12 hours. Don't worry- she made me feel plenty guilty about it. I can't believe I had to apologize to my mother for having a concussion.

Did I mention my ankle is broken? It's really painful. Depending on how my leg is suspended in the air, it changes from a dull ache to a burning pressure. This is the pits. I've never even had a sprain before. I guess when I do things, I do them all the way. Good for me. It's just too bad that I didn't do this in high school. I could have had a cast and had all my friends sign it and it would seem like I had a boyfriend maybe because all the signatures would have been from my guy friends. (What a strange thing to be thinking about. I must be on some sort of crazy pain killer. Morphine maybe?)

I am so bored right now. I almost consider cracking open that stupid book Liam brought, but my hands are so sore that I can't bear to pick it up. I think when he comes back, I'll ask if I can borrow his laptop and watch some DVD's. I bet he wouldn't mind running over to Coen's to pick up a few for me.

Oh no! Coen's! Emperor! I haven't seen him since yesterday morning. Nobody's been there to feed him or to let him out. I start panicking. What can I do about this? I can't think of what to do. No one's here to help me. The nurse. I'll page the nurse. I press the button on the side of the bed with my right knuckle (the one on my index finger- is it called my index knuckle?)

Nurse Macy shuffles in. (She shuffles alright. I think it's the most comfortable way for her to walk. She's at least 11 months pregnant from the look of things.)

"What can I do for you Shannon? Need pain medicine?" (Well, yes. Is there ever a patient who doesn't need more pain relief?)

"I do. But right now I have something a little more important on my mind. I have to get in touch with my family. I'm supposed to be dog-sitting and I haven't been there since yesterday morning. I'm really worried about him. I have to get someone to go over and feed him."

"Take a deep breath, Shannon. It's not a matter of life or death."

"To me it is. To Emperor it might be. To Coen it might be."

"Coen?"

"My friend. It's his dog. He's out of town. What if Emperor wrecks something in the house? What if he's sick?"

"Shannon, take a deep breath."

"Can you please stop worrying about my respiratory health!? Breathing is not my problem."

"Okay. What can I do to help you?"

"Can you just hand me my cell phone?"

"Your phone isn't here."

What? Oh no! It must be at work. Argh! My phone is my life line. What if Coen has texted me? What if Charlie called? Or Chance? I wouldn't want to miss a call from him either. What if Ryan has been trying to get in touch? What if Sam Haire called to ask me out again? Even that would be a crime to miss.

"Well how did my family know I was here?"

"I'm not sure. The EMT's probably got the info and passed it along at the hospital. Your work would have had contact numbers and all that for you."

She must be right.

"So, how can I get in touch with my family? Can you call them for me?"

"That's not really my job."

Oh man. What am I going to do?

She asks me another question, "How would you rate your pain level, Shannon?"

(What kind of pain? The pain in my neck is a bit much right now. And I don't mean my vertebrae.) Assuming she only wants to know about my physical pain, I answer.

"I would say it's about a 6 at this moment. It's pretty bad but it's not unbearable."

"Okay. I'm going to get the nurse on the next shift to bring you some T3's."

(Am I supposed to say thank you? Like she's doing me some kind of favor? I just can't bring myself to do it.)

"Thanks Macy," I say. (Stupid social niceties.)

She leaves my room and I'm left in this stupid bed worrying about all my stupid stuff being at stupid work and stupid Coen's dog stupid starving at his stupid house. (I definitely need a T3 and I need to get out of here.)

The only thing I can think to do stuck here in this bed, helpless and feeble, is to try and sleep. I close my eyes and try desperately to turn off my brain and sleep. Counting sheep doesn't work, humming to myself doesn't work. This is taking forever. I even briefly have a feeling like someone came into the room but I'm not sure about that. I want to stop stressing about not sleeping. So, I try to give myself something to picture that will give me sweet dreams. This turns out to be unnecessary.

"Shanny?"

"Mhmm," I say with my eyes still closed, not bothering to worry about who it is.

"Can I come in Shanny?"

"Go ahead." I don't really recognize the voice. Maybe it's the new nurse? I have a male nurse? "Do you have my T3's?"

"Nope. Unfortunately these people don't allow civilians to give drugs to patients. Even if you try to bribe the nurses with a cheque for half a mil."

Half a mil? What the heck is this guy talking about? Who is this guy? I open my eyes and turn my head towards the voice.

"Charlie Barley?" I ask in a weak voice.

"The one and only," he says with a nice soft grin. "Only, not Barley, it's Turcotte. But you, Ms. Shanny, can call me Charlie Barley anytime you like."

"I like Charlie Barley," I say. (Okay I am clearly doped up. Right? Please?)

"Good," he says. "These are for you."

He puts a bouquet of flowers on the desk thing next to my bed.

"We've got to find something to put these in," he says and looks around. "Got anything we could use?" he asks.

"No." I say bluntly. I obviously don't.

He grins sheepishly. "Be right back."

He leaves the room. Even in my possibly medicated state I feel embarrassed. I can't believe he came here! How did he know? How bad do I look? It's probably a good thing I don't have a mirror right now, I'd probably burst into tears. I feel hideous. Do I look as bad as I feel? Oh man. I can't even think something sarcastic right now. I'm just too sad. I hate this.

I've really got to get control of myself. Breathe out. Breathe out. Breathe out. Oh- breathe in. Don't forget that Shanny. He's not here to be impressed. He must have expected that I would look like a train wreck (a car wreck in this case.) Why is he here? How did he know I was here?

"I'm back," he says, "and I found the perfect vessel for those flowers." He produces a plastic pitcher, the kind they use to bring ice chips and water to the pregnant women I guess, from behind his back. He smiles like he's done something clever and mischievous and he grabs the flowers and puts them in the beige substitute vase. "You like flowers, right? That's why you were going to meet with my uncle. I asked him about it when I got back to the office the other day after we met. He said he was going to meet with you about working as a purchaser to help the designer for our new offices. Your brother had told him you were talented and just looking for a break." He looks at me and slows down. "Do you need anything?"

He sits down as he finishes this reveal. I'm not totally sure what I'm supposed to say here and I can't really look at him. I just can't.

"Shanny? Do you need anything?"

Maybe I need him to leave. I'm about to say this in a polite way but then I remember I really do need help. Can I ask him to help with this?

"I actually do need something but I don't think I can ask for your help with it. It's too- Oh wait, sorry. I wasn't thinking clearly. I've just thought of a better way you could help. Can you call my brother for me? In my rush to get here I forgot my cell phone at work-"

"Well, you didn't really forget it."

"Right, but my phone is at work and I need to get in touch with my family. I need Liam or my mom to run an important errand for me."

"I can definitely call them for you, Shanny, but why not just send me to run this errand for you?"

I am trying to figure out just who this guy is.

"Charlie, why are you offering to do errands for me? You don't even really know me. Why are you here?"

"I'm sorry, Shanny, if I'm bothering you." (It's nice, the way he says this, straight up without any self-pity. He's not looking for me to make him feel better.)

"You're not bothering me. No way are you bothering me, Charlie. The flowers are so nice- did I say thank you? Thank you. I mean, I just want to know why you're here. How did you find out about all this?" I ask, feebly gesturing to my leg and my face.

"I tried to call you yesterday to set up an appointment to meet again, but I got your voicemail three times. I left messages."

"I never got any messages," I interject before remembering that the reason I never heard those messages is the same reason why I'm lying in this bed.

He smiles nicely at me as I shake my head as I realize how lame that must sound.

"I know you didn't. My assistant called you too and left a few messages later in the day. I guess you can just erase them all without having to listen to them now." (No way. I mean I'll erase the assistant's messages without listening to them, but I have to hear what Charlie said. I am sooo curious.)

He continues, "Chance saw me later that night as I was leaving the office and asked if I'd spoken with you. When I said no, he pulled out his cell and called Liam. I think that my uncle was going to complain about being given the runaround but obviously hearing about the accident stopped him. Liam filled us in, told us what happened. I was worried about you. And so, here I am."

It makes sense actually. It definitely makes more sense than what I had been fantasizing: that Charlie sensed I was hurt and followed his instincts until they led him to my bedside where he would realize we were meant for each other. Focus, Shanny, focus. He is clearly a very thoughtful guy. And it seems like he legitimately cares. And he is good at following up on things. So, I go for it.

"Charlie," I begin with a deep breath, "how would you feel about meeting an Emperor?"

Chapter 9

Shanny is... recovering. That's what the doctor says anyway...

Charlie is my hero. He came back after less than two hours. I can tell how long it took because no matter how hard I tried to move my eyes, they stayed glued to the wall clock. (Who came up with that, by the way? Gluing your eyes to something? That's actually super gross if you stop to think about it. In fact, it's sooo gross.)

Anyway, Charlie drove to Safeway and retrieved all my stuff. (Luckily, I haul everything to work and keep it in my backpack. Not very mature, but very fortunate in this case.) Then, he went to Coen's and fed Emperor. He even took a picture of him and Emperor outside on a quick, much needed walk around the block. He showed me the picture on his cell phone. (Pretty thoughtful, right?)

I'm quite confident that he didn't snoop around Coen's place. Before he left he described himself as a good church boy. That is not the kind of thing guys in their early thirties say just to impress people, I don't think. Besides, why would Charlie dig through Coen's stuff? He knows that Coen is not my boyfriend. (I think I explained that we are 'just good friends' about ten times. Literally, ten times.) So, in the remote possibility that Charlie would snoop because he was jealous, and I know it's a very remote possibility, he would have no reason to think I have a relationship with Coen. Plus, when you add in the driving time, the walking time, the explaining time, etc., he wouldn't have had more than ten minutes to look around Coen's house for…? Well, for what, I don't really know. (I do know what I found after inadvertently digging around, but it's unlikely Charlie would care that Coen has a diamond ring, unless Charlie is some sort of secret jewel thief planning to frame me.)

At this moment, Charlie is searching through my iPod menu.

"You have terrible taste in music," he says.

I do not! "I do not!"

"Where's anything classic?"

"Do you mean classical? Like Mozart? Or are you a Brahms man?" I ask in an affected voice.

"Neither. I'm more of an Eagles man or The Stones or U2."

Wait a minute. Since when is U2 considered classic? Maybe their 80's stuff?

"Wow, Charlie. You're so edgy, so current," I say.

He laughs and puts down my iPod. He looks at me. Kind of thoughtfully. "You seem in a much better mood," he says.

"I should be. They upped my morphine." Oh- whoops. I need to make sure he knows I'm kidding. "I'm not serious. I'm not an addict."

"Now, now, Shanny, I had a feeling you had a dark terrible secret. What I mean is, I can just tell you are way calmer now that your Emperor has been fed, walked, and picked up after." This last part he says as though it reminds him of a traumatic moment in his life. What an unpredictable guy.

"I do feel a lot better. And I have you to thank for that. I wish I could hire you to take care of everything I overlook. It could be a life-long contract, with little chance of advancement, terrible pay, and little or no training."

"Are you offering me a Mcjob?"

Seriously! I have to know. Can he read my mind? Has he been stalking me for the past twenty-eight years? Or is life just way too good to me at this moment? (Well it's not the third possibility, I realize as the pain in my ankle jerks me back to reality.)

"Not offering a job so much as letting you know we may want to interview you. We'll keep your resumé on file." I try to sound jovial but I know the pan is coming through my voice.

"The pain is pretty bad huh?"

Should I pretend to be brave, the PSG's usual modas operandi? No. Where does that get me? I'm going to be honest with him.

"To me it is. I've never had anything broken before, or been so scraped up for that matter."

He doesn't respond. So, I keep talking, "Do I look as bad as I feel?"

"Well, I don't know how bad you feel. You look great for someone who's been in an accident. Don't get me wrong, you look like you've been in an accident, but you look… lucky.

"I'm not really sure what that means."

"Me neither. You know, I'm not normally so inarticulate. Being around you makes me say stupid things, I guess. Like the other day, when we met. I should have rescheduled the meeting with you right then and there. I don't know why I didn't."

Me neither.

"It's not a big deal," I say. "And you're not that inarticulate. You're just thinking out loud. You should just be glad that your out loud thoughts are more interesting than a lot of people's practiced conversation."

"That sounds kind of cynical."

"Sorry." The way he said that made me feel bad. But who did he think I was? Pollyanna? Mary Sunshine? One of the hosts from Entertainment Tonight? Well I can't pretend to be fascinated by empty talk, no matter how rich or famous the vapid vacuum may be.

"Hey, don't apologize. You have every reason to be in a bad mood," he says and taps my ankle.

"Owww!" I can't help it. That really hurt.

"Oh Shanny! I am so sorry."

Now it's my turn I guess. "You don't need to apologize. It was an accident. After all the feats you've completed for me today, I should let you get away with almost anything. Once."

He smiles appreciatively.

The night nurse comes into the room and informs Charlie that he has to leave; visiting hours for non-family members are over.

"Alright, I'll go," he says to this older woman who obviously means business.

"Thanks for coming," I say. I really mean it, for many reasons.

"You're welcome." He stretches his hand out to shake mine, then sees my bandages and realizes that a good handshake is out of the question. "Oh- sorry, Shanny. Again!"

"Charlie, don't even worry about it." (That doesn't really sound like me. Who have I heard saying that trite sentence before? I can't remember.)

"Well, I'll see you tomorrow," he says and gets up to leave.

Tomorrow? "Tomorrow?"

"Sure, if I can get here, I will see you tomorrow. If not, I'll be by later this week. But I'll try to see you tomorrow. Good night Shanny."

"Good night, Charlie Barley," I say somewhat wistfully I think, as he leaves and the nurse closes the door.

Charlie might have to work to clear his schedule, but he did say he'd come to see me tomorrow. I didn't think it was worth mentioning that I would see him earlier than that- in about as much time as it takes to close my eyes and start dreaming.

Good night, Charlie Barley.

Chapter 10

Shanny is… "a kind and generous soul… in bed."

It's true. My fortune cookie told me. And unlike horoscopes, fortune cookies are never wrong. (Okay fine, they're often wrong. But it is possible that I am a kind and generous soul. It is possible.)

Mmmm. I love Chinese Food. And I love Ryan for bringing me this food. It's from her favorite Chinese restaurant, Leong Kwan's, which happens to be owned by Koreans and their head chef is Thai. (Mmmm, Thai food. That will be for tomorrow.) I prefer the Perfect Prawn Palace- they have the best fried rice and they always give me an extra egg roll, as though I am a preferred customer.

Unfortunately, all this pain medication has left me feeling pretty groggy and I can't eat as much as I'd like and it doesn't taste as good as it could. Ryan is clearly enjoying it.

"Isn't this the best fried rice you've ever had?" she asks me.

"It's pretty great," I say as I finish about all I can eat.

"You're full?" she asks as though this has never happened before. (Which definitely has happened before and she knows it.)

"Yeah, I think so. I've eaten lots and Dr. Shoker has warned me not to eat too much junk food until-"

"It's not junk food!"

"Well, of course not, but you know what I mean. I shouldn't be eating anything fried or whatever."

"Oh. Okay." (She seems a little less offended.)

"I'm actually expecting Dr. Shoker at any minute."

"Dr. Shoker? Is he Indian?"

"She is. She's Punjabi."

"How interesting."

I just can't stand the sickeningly sweet way she says this. Who cares where your doctor's from as long as they're trained, respectful, and doing their job? Not me.

"Yeah. She's great. Really funny."

"I don't know that being funny is a quality that makes a doctor great, Shanny."

"It's better than not being funny. And as far as I'm concerned, and I am the girl in the hospital gown, it is a great quality." (Have I shared my thoughts on hospital gowns? It's probably not worth it; likely they are the same as those had by any gal, perpetually single or not. Maybe Lulu Lemon could start a line of hospital clothes- they'd be cute, functional, and they would definitely cheer me up.)

Ryan changes the topic to one more reasonable and relevant. "So, why is this Dr. Shoker coming to see you? Are you being released?"

"I don't think so. Not yet. Soon probably." (I can't believe I never noticed this before but Ryan can really wolf down an egg roll. It's like, well, picture a fat kid inhaling a Twinkie. It's like that- Asian style.)

She keeps talking even with her mouth full. Eww, partially chewed bean sprouts. "What are you going to do when you get out of here, Shanny?" she asks me. "Has this been a wakeup call?"

I'm sorry?

"I wasn't aware I needed a wakeup call, Ryan."

"Come on, Shanny. Be serious. You're going to be thirty in a couple of years, you work at Safeway, and you live in a terrible apartment. You're single."

And you're a nosy, egg-roll munching cow, you stupid-

"How is our Shanny, Today?"

Ryan is so freaking lucky that Dr. Shoker came in when she did. Sooo lucky. I swear I would have said out loud exactly what I think of Ryan and her assessment of my "terrible, in need of a wakeup call" life.

"I'm pretty good, Dr. Shoker. I should have followed your advice and stayed away from eating this junk," I say gesturing to the Styrofoam vessels of msg. (Take that Ryan!)

"Probably anything is better than hospital food but next time you need an Asian fix, I suggest Thai, less hard on the tummy."

(Oh man. Dr. Shoker saying the word tummy? I am old! I don't need pediatric wing terminology. Grow up Dr. Shoker.)

She goes on, "I mean it's better for digestion and for heart burn as long as it's not too spicy." (Uh oh. Did she read my mind? Hopefully, she didn't read it from my face. I've really got to get a handle on the facial muscle intentional look thing.)

"Thai food is too spicy," says Ryan.

(Yes, Ryan. Cows cannot handle spicy food. Though dairy products are excellent for helping alleviate their burning effects.)

Dr. Shoker nods with an odd smile and drums her fingers on my chart. Is it terrible to admit that I keep waiting for her beats to turn into full blown Bollywood numbers? Like she'll spin around and some guys will come in singing their undying love to her only to be interrupted by a stream of girls in brightly colored Indian suits dancing and smiling way too huge. Then her father will come in and forbid her to marry the man of her dreams because he is only a poor hair gatherer. (Either I need to stop watching Bollywood movies or I need to stop eating funky food while on pain meds. Or maybe I need to do more of both.)

"Well, I need to speak with Shanny on an important matter."

"That's not a problem for me," Ryan says.

"It's a problem for me," I say.

"Shanny!"

"Seriously, Ryan. Who knows what this is about? Maybe I need privacy."

"Fine," she says, "I will wait outside. You just call if you need me, Shanny." She slings her purse over her arm, grabs her cell phone, and starts texting (Brian probably.) I never knew someone who's been asked to leave a room who walks out so importantly. She definitely thinks she owns the room. But she doesn't. The taxpayers own this room. (At least until everything gets privatized- then, maybe she can own it, but not yet.)

Dr. Shoker looks at me quizzically. "You're friends with her?"

I pause. "Yup."

"Alright then."

I shift myself up in the bed and toss the Styrofoam Ryan left on my sheets over on to the plastic thing posing as a chair next to me. Miss. Eugh. Epic miss. It lands on the floor not even bothering to announce its traumatic encounter with gravity with sound. No wonder I don't play basketball. Does Dr. Shoker play basketball? Do Indian doctors have time to play basketball? Do any doctors? It probably has nothing to do with ethnicity. You know what does have to do with ethnicity? Genetics. Oh no. Genetics- genetic diseases. Maybe that's why she needs to talk to me. I have some kind of horrible genetic disease that afflicts Irish girls who are nearly twenty-nine (ish) and have terrible lives with nothing to show for, for anything.

"What's wrong with me?" I ask.

"Pardon?"

"Just tell me. I'm old. I can handle it. What am I dying of? Is it bad? Will it be painful? Give it to me straight." (Never mind Bollywood movies, I need to avoid old 1930's melodramas, avoid them like the plague. Oh, I hope I don't have the plague.)

"The only things wrong with you Shanny, are the outcomes of the accident. Your foot, your ribs, your face."

My face? Ouch.

"I mean the scrapes etc. All of which you will heal from I predict. Your internal structures are all working great."

Ooh- a medical compliment.

"So what is it then? What do you need to talk to me about? I thought it must be serious since Ryan had to leave."

"It is serious. It's just not bad."

"Okay. Hit me."

"Well, as I said, this is a serious thing. You really have to think about it."

This is killing me. Think about what?

"Before you woke up, while you were unconscious, we checked over your information and you are registered as an organ donor."

"But I didn't die." Isn't organ donation just harvesting salvageable parts from dead people?

"I know that, Shanny. Organ donation isn't only a procedure performed on dead donors. Live donors are a major part of donation."

Okay, so I was wrong. What a moron.

"So, you want my organs? What, my liver? A kidney?"

"No such thing, Shanny." Dr. Shoker says and then does something incomprehensible she moves towards me, curls her fingers and speaks in a crazy Indian/Transylvanian accent. "Ve vant your blood."

"What?"

She looks at me and stands up straight again.

"You have good blood Shanny. Anyway, we've done some tests and we've actually found that you are a close genetic match to a young boy in this hospital. This really almost never happens Shanny."

(She's excited by this. Huh.)

"Anyway, he has Leukemia and you happen to be a close match. Your human leukocyte antigen tissue type is compatible with his."

"My what?"

"Your human leukocyte antigen markers. But don't worry about that. Just call it your HLA if it comes up."

"And these HLA things matter for?"

"For bone marrow transplants. The chances are abnormally high that you match this boy and could be a donor for him. Your donation could make a major difference."

Like I could save his life?

"You could help save his life potentially Shanny."

"I'll do it."

"Your enthusiasm is great. We just have to talk over the risks, which are really minimal, and the details of the procedure. Then you can decide if you really want to do this. You can always change your mind."

"I won't change my mind."

I won't. I listen to Dr. Shoker's explanations. This doesn't sound that bad. There's no cost to me. It isn't a long procedure. (And really, since I'm stuck here recovering from this stupid thoughtless accident, who cares? I'm here anyway.) And the oh-so-frightening potential side effects? Lower back pain. Fatigue. Stiffness when walking. Bleeding at the collection site. Oh no. Save me from these evil demons. Don't even bother me about that nonsense- nonsense! (I have so many pain centers to complain about, that adding those would be like shaking table salt into the ocean- entirely pointless and stupid.)

I smile and nod through her whole spiel.

"So, what's next?" I ask.

"Well, I'm going to take a cheek swab and run a couple more tests just to ensure we have the best possible match here and it's all worthwhile."

"Swab away," I say. Eww. That sounded sooo gross.

Luckily, Dr. Shoker chooses to ignore it.

"Well, I've got all I need. I'll be by to see you tomorrow about all this. Make sure you talk to you family about it. They need to know it's your choice. You'll need their support."

Oh yes. I always need the kind of support they give.

"It's only six, but I'll say it anyway, good night, Shanny."

"Good night, Dr. Shoker."

She opens the door and runs into Ryan.

Has she been waiting out there this whole time? Man, go home, crazy! Get a life.

I shouldn't be so mean, I know, but I need some alone time. I just want to be alone, have some time to think before my mom comes for her unnecessary nightly vigil.

"I insist you go home now," says Dr. Shoker. "Shanny has been given lots of pain meds. She won't be coherent for very long."

"What do you mean? She's coherent now. I can see her."

"Thy drugs are quick," The doctor tells Ryan and magically on cue, my eyes "become" heavy and I moan a little bit. "You see? She'll be out for hours. Good bye."

She turns off the light in my room for added drama before closing the door. I do not see Ryan (my friend Ryan, I have to remember, my friend Ryan who cared enough to bring me Chinese food) for the rest of the night.

Dr. Shoker, I love you. In a professional doctor-patient way. Now if only you could have someone come in here and clear out all this smelly Chinese food.

Chapter 11

Shanny is... feeling like her life is a Wes Anderson movie- only not funny.

Connor Hardy- But Shan, no Wes Anderson movie is funny.

Ryan Cooper-Kokozka- I agree with you Connor. Not funny.

Shanny Hardy- What?! At least admit Rushmore was good.

Connor Hardy- nope.

Muriel Hardy- Shannon, who is Wes Anderson? Does he live in your building?

Today is the day before The Day. Surgery (sort of a hyperbolic word to me now) is scheduled for tomorrow morning. Tests are mostly done. All is well and all I need to do is try and relax. (Try, Shanny, try.) We're just waiting for Dr. Shoker to return from running one last test. The waiting is not what is stressing me out. My mother is doing that all on her own.

"This is interesting Shanny. Listen to this." (Oh please no, please stop.)

Of course, my mother doesn't stop. She peers over the pages of the torturous book Liam bought for me. "I mean it Shanny, listen to what he writes, 'emotionally healthy women attract emotionally healthy men.' Now that's true. Do you want me to highlight it for you?"

"Mom. Did you bring a highlighter to my hospital room?" (What for? To tag my leg in case they try to swap me with someone else in the recovery room?)

"Oh. No, I don't have a highlighter," she says sadly as she rummages through her purse. "Why don't I just fold the page for you? Or I could use this pen and underline the lines I think you need to read?"

What an offer! Why don't you just make broad expressive circles around all the content on all the pages? I am going to have to take drastic measures. I am going to have to get out of this stupid bed and grab that stupid book and throw it in the stupid garbage. (And then cover it with something else- I wouldn't put it past my mother to take the book out of the garbage. Then lecture me about my stubborn refusal to accept positive help from my family.)

Hang on- the solution here is not quite so crazy.

"Mom," I say in my most pleasant, good daughter voice, "if you are loving this book so much, why don't you take it home and finish it? I don't mind."

She narrows her eyebrows. "I just thought I would read it out loud to you while you are stuck here for the next few days and then when you go back to your house you can pick up where we finish off."

Oh, I'm finished. For sure.

She keeps reading, sharing those unsolicited pearly gems of wisdom. All I can do at this point is tilt my head back and take a deep breath. (Try, Shanny, try.) Oh, hey! I know what will make me feel a little better! I turn over (ow) and look towards the door at my beautiful lemon tree.

Charlie dropped it off last night. He looked so funny hauling in this mini tree in its heavy silvery circular pot. He was pretty much out of breath. I have to say I like the little tree (I like the delivery boy even more.) It is a little strange though that he would give me a lemon tree- what is that all about?

He said he thought it would smell good and the sales girl assured him that as long as it is taken care of properly, it will grow and have fruit. When I looked skeptical, he reminded me that someone as enthusiastic about flowers as myself should be more than able of nurturing a Dwarf Meyer Lemon tree. Of course I can do it! (Or I could just give it to Kim. It can keep my orchid company.)

I'm beginning to worry that Charlie sees me as some sort of Earth mother with, what he considers to be, sub-par taste in music. I'm going to be a big letdown. (By the way, let down, bring down? Why all the negative connotation with the direction down?) But if he wants to keep coming around, smiling at me, and bringing me thoughtful gifts, who am I to object?

Mom has been rattling for a few minutes now and I've had it.

"A smoothie. Mom, would you go and get me a fruit smoothie?"

"Pardon, Shanny?"

My bad manners might offend her as much as the interruption.

"I can't eat anything as of five pm or something and I don't really feel like I can eat the hospital food."

She doesn't look convinced. Time for the big guns. "Connor told me the smoothies down there are organic. He said they were delicious."

"Alright, Shannon." She grabs her wallet and pulls out a ten. "What flavor would you like?" she asks as she heads to the door

"Something with strawberries please. Other than that I'm easy."

"Alright. Oh! Hello, Conrad." she says.

"Hello, Mrs. Hardy. You're going down to pick something up? Would you like me to do that for you?" (He is such a charmer.)

"You know, you are just the nicest of Shanny's friends. No dear, you go and sit down."

Honestly. This guy. He needs to shave. Rather, he could use a shave but I always think he looks pretty good with the stubble look- like he could be in a Hugo Boss ad. He puts down his laptop case and kisses me on the top of the head.

"How are you, Shanny?"

"Oh, ya know. Just hangin' out. Relaxin'. Seriously, I'll be okay."

"Good. Did I just hear you tell your mother you were easy? That's news to me."

Typical. After one moment of sincere emotion and concern, he goes right back to mocking me. This is part of what I hate/love about Coen.

"News to me too. How was your trip? How's Emperor?"

"Don't know about the dog. Haven't been home yet. But your mom called me while she was at my house feeding him. She was worried he wasn't getting enough protein in his diet. I told her she could feed him a steak from the freezer."

"I'll bet she did."

"Sometimes sarcasm just doesn't register through the phone."

"So how was the trip then? How was Paris?"

"Paris," he says in a French accent, "was the beautiful city of lights. And a good place to find this." He says as he grandly unzips his laptop case and pulls out a beautiful Hermes scarf. Normally, I would shrink from buying something with this type of print (or this type of price) but this blue and purple number is gorgeous- not really me- but still gorgeous. I tie it on where my neck brace used to be.

"How does it look? Hospital chic?"

"It's great huh? Val helped me pick it out."

Sound unaffected Shanny. "She did a great job."

"She did. She is great. I had a great time with her."

Great.

He keeps on, "It's maybe the first time I got why people call Paris the city of love."

Even more great.

I start untying the scarf. "I don't want it to get dirty."

It's like he didn't even hear me. "Did you hear me, Shanny? I think I may be in love."

This is a really big deal and I have to think of just the perfect thing to say in reply.

"That's great. I'm having surgery tomorrow."

"Surgery?"

"Yes. I'm donating my bone marrow."

"You're doing what?"

I talk deliberately slowly. "I'm donating my bone marrow."

"I heard you. What are you doing that for?"

What kind of a question is that? Why is he zipping up his case in that jerky way?

"I'm doing it because it's a good thing to do. I'm going to help save a kid's life."

"That's a bit dramatic, Shan."

"No, it's not."

There is a very awkward silence. I don't know if Coen and I have ever had an awkward silence between us. This is awkward.

"Anyway, the surgery is tomorrow morning. I should be going home in just a couple of days. They usually let you go home the same day as a bone marrow donation but since I'm already in recovery, Dr. Shoker wants me to stay here a bit longer."

Coen sits down on the edge of my bed. He's shaking his head. "I don't think you should do this, Shanny. It's not a good idea. It's not safe."

"It's very safe actually. It's not a risky procedure."

"Neither is walking in a parking lot for most people. But you are an accident waiting to happen."

"That's not true. I'm an accident that just happened. I'm free and clear for a while." I sit up to try to make my point even stronger but wind up pulling my side, which my ribs do not appreciate. "Ow!"

"You see, Shanny? That's what I mean. You're a mess. You're hurt. Look at your ankle. Look at your face. Now is not the time you should be having a risky operation."

"It is not risky. What is your problem?"

"I don't have a problem. I'm just worried for you. I'm telling you not to do this."

"And who are you?"

"Excuse me?"

"Who are you to me to tell me what I can or can't do? You're not my doctor. You're not my family. You're not my husband or my boyfriend-"

"I'm your friend Shanny."

I am on a roll now. "Right. You're my friend. We have fun. We support each other. We don't tell each other what to do with our lives. So don't tell me what to do."

"You don't have to get so angry."

"You don't have to be here."

"Just calm down, Shanny," he says rolling his eyes.

(Somehow I always believed that Coen was smart enough never to tell a girl to calm down. I guess not.)

"I don't want to be around you right now. And since I can't get up from this bed, you're going to have to walk out the door."

"You're throwing me out?" he says, almost yelling.

Now who's being dramatic?

"Coen, I have enough people in my life telling me what to do or that I'm wrong about everything, but no one has doubted me on this. My family is proud of me for doing this. And no, that's not why I'm doing it. But they're proud of me. I don't need your support- I have theirs. Heck, I even have Ryan's. And Lucy told me I was her hero. So, you can have your stupid bad attitude and go home to your dog."

And your girlfriend. And that engagement ring in the kitchen door.

He shakes his head. "I'm just being honest. I think you're making a mistake, Shanny. Do you even know the kid you're donating to? You don't do you?"

"It doesn't matter. What? If he was a Nobel laureate he would be worthy of my marrow? Or maybe the next winner of So You Think You Can Dance? Or the next Prime Minister?" I pause to take a deep breath. "I'm supposed to stay calm. See you."

He picks up his bag. He looks baffled. Maybe he's jet lagged. Could that be an excuse for our irrational fight- jet lag and hospital fumes?

"I hope it works out," he says in an obnoxious/predicting-the-opposite tone.

"It will."

"I hope so," he says and leaves.

Resisting the urge to be dramatic and slam the door, he closes it softly, remembering he's in a hospital probably. I watch the door close. My eye catches the lemon tree. My lemon tree. From Charlie. Then I look down at the scarf I am practically choking out in my hands. (Was I doing that while Coen was here? Eugh. That would be pretty rude. Poor little scarf. Little scarf that cost more than my iPod probably.)

I wish I could shift my bed over next to the lemon tree so that I could pet it. No I don't. I wish I could get the tree to magically send a psychic message to Charlie. Something like, "Come quick. Shanny has hurt feelings. And she looks really good right now. And she doesn't care about who went to Paris with whom." (Maybe strike the last two parts- I wouldn't want the tree to be involved in a lie.)

Mom comes back in the room, interrupting my strange little fantasy. She is sipping from a super pink smoothie. She hands me something an off putting beige-ish colour.

"They ran out of strawberry."

(Of course they did.)

"I got you banana/kiwi. Now, what page were we on before I left?"

Chapter 12

Shanny is… getting out tomorrow.

Hallelujah! It's true. Tonight will be my last night in this 5 star Universal Health care Hell. I don't mean to sound ungrateful. The surgery was smooth sailing. The doctors have been pretty great and the nurses have (mostly) been helpful. I just really can't wait to watch a movie on my TV instead of on Liam's lap top.

I might miss the drugs though. This whole thing has been pretty painful. My body is tired, puffy, and banged up- more from the accident than from the surgery. (The surgery has just made me feel stiff and lying on my side is not my reclining posture of choice.) I am facing the door right now just praying for someone to come in and talk to me. (I would even let mom come in as long as she doesn't read that hideously preachy book at me- and I mean <u>at</u> me not to me.)

Like magic, my will materializes into my dreamy guy- Charlie comes through the door with a smile that's somehow mischievous and sincere at the same time. His hair is perfect and he is wearing some kind of great pinstripe suit. What does he do really? I know he works for his uncle but he must do something pretty official to be dressed like this on a Wednesday.

I can feel the flush on my face, it's like my smile is some sort of involuntary reflex, like hammer on knee equals kick; sour lemonade equals head shake; Charlie's face equals giddy grin.

"Are you just coming from work?" I ask. (Oh no I sound groggy- and not in a sexy way- in a chain-smoking-phlegm-stuck-in-my-throat way.)

"Kind of," he says and walks over to the sink. He fills one of those little plastic Dixie cups with water and brings it over to me.

I say thanks and try to be demure as I sip it. Of course I spill.

"I was working on a project," he says "Inspired by you, actually."

"Really?"

"Yes, Shanny," he says as he pulls the wheely stool towards the bed and sits on it. He pulled it with a bit too much gusto and he slides right into the bed with a bump.

"Sorry," he says. His face is really close to mine. Could this be a kissable moment? No- I am gross. I haven't brushed my teeth since last night. And it smells like he had a little too much garlic for lunch or dinner.

"That's alright. So, tell me what your project is."

"It's a pretty big deal."

"Uh huh?"

"I would say it was major."

"Major? Like what? Like you have finally decided to listen to music written after the mid-90's?"

"Never," he says with a twinkle in his eye. (Bad breath or not- I would kiss him back.)

"So, what is it?"

"I have decided to go to Peru for two months."

"What?" (How exactly was this inspired by me?)

"I've joined a volunteer organization. I asked my uncle for the time off and he said yes. So, I, like you Shanny, *(oh what a difference a comma makes!)* am going to do something good for the world."

He thinks I did something good for the world? "You think I did something good for the world?"

He squeezes my hand and nods like the question wasn't even worth asking.

"Well, I'm glad," I say, "that you think that. Not everyone does."

"Not everyone matters," he says.

I consider this for a minute. Somehow the way he says it isn't cruel, it is life-affirming and wonderful. Never mind what what's-his-name said.

"So, what are you going to be doing for the people of Peru?" I ask.

"I'm going to be teaching kids to play soccer."

Huh? "Really?"

"Yes. There's an organization here that fundraises and sends volunteers down to help the kids there learn to play soccer."

"So, a bunch of preppy Canadian boys are going to teach Peruvian kids to play soccer-football?"

"Yes- exactly."

"Isn't that like traveling to China to teach people how to make fried rice?" (Unnecessary, presumptuous, stupid-)

"Well, no. It's awesome."

"Do you even play soccer, I mean football?" (Oh no. His feelings look hurt. Why do I have to say all these things?)

"I do, Shanny."

"Are you good?" (Shut up Shanny!)

He sits back a ways from me. "I'm not bad."

"I mean, I'm sure you are. Good, I mean. I just, I wasn't thinking. This trip sounds great. And I'm sure the kids will appreciate having someone there who cares enough to make such a trip."

His smile gets a little wider.

I continue, "And if you are bringing new balls I'll bet they never leave you alone. They'll follow you around everywhere I bet. I think that's great."

He's nodding.

"So, when do you leave?" I ask.

"Tomorrow."

"Tomorrow?" (Ack!)

"Yes. That's why I had to come by tonight. I finished up my work, ran over to the travel agent *(who uses a travel agent nowadays? Hello-internet?)*, and came over here to wish you goodbye."

Oh no. Good bye. Two months in Peru will definitely be enough time for him to forget about me, even if I am his inspiration.

"Okay then," I say. "Have a great trip, Charlie. Good bye."

"You take care, Shanny." He gets up and heads for the door. That's that I guess. I decide I will not cry until he leaves.

Just before he walks out the door he stops and points to the little lemon tree. "Take care of that. I'm expecting to be drinking fresh lemonade on your porch when I get back." He smiles and leaves.

My heart does flips. Well it tries to do flips and round-offs, like some sort of Olympic heart, but it's out of practice so it actually does some sort of cartwheel that turns into a body rolling sideways doing summersaults down the hill. Such a clumsy heart. But at least it's awake now.

Somehow though, I am falling asleep.

I'm not sure how much later it is, but I wake up to the sound of my door closing loudly. Rude. Don't people know this is a hospital? I blink myself up. Hey. There's something on my tray table thing. I kind of pull myself up. So weird. There's a rose and an envelope. Wait. Nope. Make that two envelopes. I must see what's inside.

Huh. That's funny. There are no names on the envelopes but I am going to assume that they are meant for me. I pick up the rose and sniff it before I open the envelopes. It doesn't really smell like anything. Or maybe it's just that the smell of hospital has just invaded my nostrils and just will not go away. (I picture tiny grey-white molecules on the hunt for germs floating through the room, waving their arms frantically as though they're doing the breast stroke.)

Disappointed, I put the rose back down on the tray and pick up the first envelope. Maybe there will be a name inside. But the envelope is pretty thin- it doesn't feel like there's a card. Eugh. I never understood why people owned letter openers but I think maybe I do now. Being weak and trying to rip open a closed envelope is surprisingly difficult when you've been weakened by surgery, injury and drugs. (It also doesn't help that my hands are still pretty scraped up. I mean, they're healing but they're still not one hundred percent.)

So, I bite the corner. (That helped!) Now I easily finish tearing it.

Huh.

Inside is a cheque.

Huh.

I reach in and carefully pull it out. (The last thing I need is a paper cut.)

No way.

No way.

No way.

I shake my head. I rub my eyes. I turn the cheque upside down. It doesn't look like a joke or a forgery. Can this be real? In front of me there is a cashier's cheque for fifteen thousand dollars. Fifteen thousand dollars! Made out to me! Made out to Shannon Hardy. Someone has given me a cheque for fifteen thousand dollars. Who? Who gave this to me? There is no signature.

The only logo on the cheque is at the top. In the corner it says AnonymousGiving.org. What is that? A website for philanthropists? The only information on the paper is my information, the amount, and a phone number for the bank to call when cashing in the money. In any case, the real giver is anonymous. This is crazy. Who would give me a cheque for fifteen thousand dollars?

I look back inside the envelope. Nope, nothing there. But on the back of the cheque there is a little message. It says, "For what you did."

For what I did? Oh. This is for- Oh.

Still no name.

I do not know how to feel about this.

Hold on- What could be in the other envelope?

It's skinny too, but it jingles when I open it (with my teeth again.) There is another note. It says, "thank you." But there is still no name. This is maddening. What is going on? In the envelope there are two quarters and a twenty dollar bill. What is happening here?

Could it be from the same person? Are they giving me such a huge sum of money but they worry that I can't cash the cheque in the hospital so they thought they should give me some emergency cash for now? (Like what- they think I might see something I want to buy in the gift shop? Or maybe they think I need cab fare?)

I really don't know what to think. Am I just having a hallucination?

I pinch myself (because isn't that the standard thing to do? In musicals, in songs, in old movies, in new movies, people are always asking someone to pinch them.) I am awake. This is going to keep me up all night. This is crazy.

Think of what I could do with this money. No. I can't even start. I can't take this money. I shouldn't take this money. Should I? Something about this just seems wrong. The only thing I'm sure of is that I am not telling my family. I'm not telling anyone about this. At least, not yet.

Chapter 13

Shanny is… getting back into the swing of things.

I don't really know if I ever was in the swing of things. (How high does this swing go? Is it a full blown under duck? Or an empty swing creepily, squeakily rocking in the wind?)

My swing style seems to be an empty swing in a playground full of idiot children. Well, not all the children are idiots. I just mean that there is kinetic energy blasting around me- like dynamic swooshes of colour- but I'm still in the middle of it, all my edges are clearly defined and broad.

At least I'm at the park. (Maybe that's what I am. I'm not in the swing of things- I'm just hangin' out at the park.)

Well, really, I'm at the scene of the crime. Come on, Shanny, you can do it. You can get out of the car. You can walk to the entrance. You can go to work.

I exhale for an insane amount of time. (I do have great lung capacity.) I turn the engine off. (I consider playing some kind of loud psych myself up song like Dwight on 'The Office,' but I am nowhere as cool as him. So, I just turn it off.)

I open the door, close it, lock it, and head through the parking lot of death to the store of mystery. (I wish I worked at a store of mystery.) No one notices my grand entrance, which is just the way I like it- most of the time. I drop off my stuff and head to the battlefield. Cash register number three. Apparently, I am on a solo mission this afternoon- no Lucy in sight. I wish she was here. She always has good stories and (even more importantly) she makes me feel like I have good stories.

But no such luck. No partner in crime today.

Today I am left alone with my thoughts, my memories, my back pain, and my dilemma. I left the hospital three weeks ago. My injuries are healing. I still have not cashed the cheque. I could say I haven't even looked at it, but that would be a lie. I have looked at it. And looked at it. And looked at it. I probably have the entire thing memorized. As if it turned into Braille, I can run my fingers over the cheque and feel the words coming to life. Fifteen thousand dollars. Oh man. That is sooo much money.

I've tried to find out who sent the money to me, but AnonymousGiving.org will not reveal any information- apparently it's in their manifesto. (Who has a manifesto? Should I get one?) So, I have a little list in my head, but most of them I've crossed off. Here's the list:

Charlie - no - he wouldn't be secretive about it. He already is doing something because of my inspiration. And he told me all about that.

Liam- no- he doesn't have that kind of money. (None of my brothers do.)

Mom- no- she would use the money to buy me a husband (she wouldn't trust me to know what to do with fifteen thousand dollars.)

Dr. Shoker- no- that just seems nuts.

The marrow organization center people- no- they don't have fifteen thousand dollars to give away. (And think of the precedent it would set!)

Coen- no- he made it pretty clear how he felt about the whole thing. (Like I deserved a kick in the butt, not some serious bank.)

Ryan- I don't think so. But maybe she and Brian have secret millions. She was kind of my number one fan in this whole thing.

So, my best guess is this: the parents of whoever received my bone marrow. (That makes sense, right? Who else could it be?)

So, if that's right how can I even think of taking the money? I just- it feels tainted. Like as if my good deed won't count. But I can't throw it away. (The one thing

AnonymousGiving.org would tell me is that they inform the giver when the cheque has been cashed and that if the cheque isn't cashed within two months, they contact the recipient by mail until they get a response. I do not want to be contacted by mail. That is the worst! Stacks of unopened envelopes torturing me in my own house? No thank you!)

These ideas are what run through my mind during this first day back at work.

Everything goes along like a mundane day in the trenches. Price check on a block of cheese missing its sticker, re-swipe a sticky debit card, punch in phone numbers for people who didn't bring their club cards- the usual.

Then.

It happened.

She appeared.

Why is she in my line? There are two other cashiers working! Keep walking lady, keep walking. Keep walking. No- don't stop here. Ack!

Midway through handing back the receipt to the guy in front of me (who is sporting a greasy Ron Burgundy mustache, by the way) I see her, the devil in plastic rain wear. (And it is not raining. It's July for Pete's sake. And that rain gear is not even cute.)

I freeze. Ron Burgundy sees me standing there still as a stupid statue. I imagine I hear him say "yoink" as he grabs the receipt out of my hand. But I don't watch. My eyes are fixed on the angel of death, the harbinger of traffic accidents, the plague of public transportation, the enemy of all oranges. The old woman!

I must have been still for a few minutes because now the old woman is tapping the rubber divider on the conveyor belt.

"Young lady!" she yells. "Young lady! I do not have all day. Please be about your business. Scan my items."

I am having an out-of-body experience. I can't move. I'm frozen with friggin' madness. The old woman is now waving the divider in front of my face.

"Are you alright?" someone in line behind her asks but I don't answer.

"I need a manager!" calls the bag lady (by which I mean the old woman of course.) "Manager! Manager!"

Her calling out must have been pretty vehement because the tiny woman uses the divider as a weapon and suddenly- bam! She hits me in the face.

I go into knee-jerk reflex mode. Not lemon-sour face mode. Not Charlie smile mode. This time it's get-hit-in-the-face-grab-rubber-divider-pull-it-from-old-woman's-hand-and-smack-her-on-the-shoulder reaction. I unfreeze as my eyebrows rocket to new heights. What have I done?

"Shanny!"

I turn around. Doug, my manager/art history PhD candidate, is staring at me like I spat on a Rembrandt or like I cut up a Picasso and rearranged the pieces so it actually looks like what it was meant to look like. Basically, I've committed blasphemy.

"Shanny, what did you just do?" he yells and pulls the divider out of my hand.

"I don't know," I say, kind of stunned, the divider still in my hand.

"This young lady assaulted me!" cries the old bag and she starts to whimper.

Unbelievable. Now the couple behind her is patting her on the arm comforting her, staring at me like I just killed a puppy.

Doug looks shell-shocked. "Shanny, I think you need to apologize to her right now."

"An apology is not enough!" cries the grand madam of overacting. "She should be disciplined! Fired!"

This is it for me. "Fired? Lady, you're not going to get me fired after you almost got me killed!"

Doug looks at me like I've gone completely crazy. I have to explain as quickly as I can.

"That's the lady. That's the woman who made me carry her oranges outside. And then I got hit by the car. It was her fault. And she gave me the finger and swore at me. That's why I was distracted. It's her fault I got hit. She is the reason I almost could have died." I look at her. "You crazy lad. You should be fired! From this store. Doug, tell her she can't come back to the store! *(Okay maybe I've gone nuts.)* Or tell her to apologize to me!"

"You need to calm down Miss," says the man soothing the old woman.

(Yet another male making the mistake of telling a woman to calm down. And "Miss?" Who calls me Miss?)

I look at Doug expectantly. He pulls up the phone at my station and pages another teller to come to my station. He turns to the customers and says, "I am so sorry about this. I apologize. We will sort this out right away."

I see Debbie coming to the cashier counter. Darn that stupid Debbie. Always interfering. Always coming when paged. I just hate her. She didn't even sign my get well card. Come to think of it- all Doug did was sign his name; he didn't even write a heart-warming comment. Only Lucy wrote something sincere. The rest of these people all hate me. They are against me.

"Come with me, Shanny," Doug says with an edge to his voice that makes me clench my jaw. "Now."

See? Against me!

As Doug escorts me away, I hear a mix of clapping, and voices reassuring the old orange saboteur that I'm gone and I won't be coming back. Didn't they see her hit me? Don't they know she is guilty of almost-murder? (Well, almost-murder-by-accident...) Why isn't anyone on my side here? Lucy!

"Lucy!" I say desperately. "Lucy saw that old woman. She knows I'm right! Call Lucy! Doug, call Lucy."

We are in the break room now. Just Doug and me. I hate this. He is sitting on the edge of the table. His posture is that of a high school principal trying to be cool and effective as he tells troublesome teens that he is disappointed in them. (Not that such a thing ever happened to me…)

"Shanny," he says after a deflated sigh, "maybe you came back to work too soon. You're still not doing great, I guess. Are you still on meds?"

What does that have to do with anything? What right does he have to ask such a question? That must be against some labor law. We're in Canada! I refuse to answer.

"You aren't happy here are you, Shanny?" he asks me condescendingly. "I mean, you weren't doing all that well before the accident. You'd been here, what? Ten months?"

"Fourteen."

"Right."

"That's more than a year, Doug."

"Right, Shanny, that's what I'm getting at. You've been here over a year and you're not really doing all that well, are you?"

What the heck does that mean? I am fighting the urge to clench my fists.

"I think I'm doing pretty good," I say.

Doug shakes his head at me. "Shanny, I have problems with you all the time."

All the time? This is news to me!

"You know you forget codes, you've left the store without permission *(one time with that crazy old lady!)*, and now there's been another run in with customers. I just wonder whether working here is a good fit for you."

"Just say what you want to say, Doug," I say, my nostrils flailing and my eyes rolling, I'm sure.

"Maybe you're done here, Shanny."

"Are you firing me?" I ask slowly, deliberately, overly articulately.

"No. No," he says. 'I'm not firing you."

"Then what are you doing?"

"I'm just suggesting that maybe you should look for a new place. Maybe Safeway isn't a good fit for you."

"Why not?" I ask. "Why is Safeway not a good fit for me?"

"I don't really know what you want me to say here, Shanny."

Shut up. How about that's what I want you to say- nothing.

He goes on, "Do you want me to say you're incompetent?"

Incompetent? "Incompetent? I am not incompetent! If I were, I would have been let go a long time ago."

"Well-"

"And who is too incompetent to work at Safeway? *(Slow down, Shanny. Don't let him answer what he might answer.)* I mean it's Safeway! Debbie is your employee of the month! She got a DUI and lost her license! I know for a fact that some of the stock boys play Campbell soup can bowling right behind your back. And you're the assistant manager! I mean give me a break, Doug. You are-"

"Shanny-"

"Yeah. I know. I'll get my stuff. I'm out of here." I grab my stuff and head out the door back to my car, back to my apartment.

What did I just do?

Chapter 14

Shanny is... not in the mood.

I am officially at a new low. I can't believe I dragged my saggy butt all the way over here. What am I doing here? I should go.

And yet I keep knocking.

"Open the door Coen!" I call as I pull the spoon out of my mouth. "I know you're home! You would never just leave your car in the driveway Open the door!"

Suddenly, I regret ordering him to come. I realize how ridiculous I must appear. I look down to make sure my shirt isn't tucked into my Lulu Lemons and that my Lulu Lemons aren't tucked into my shoe or my walking cast. Some melting ice cream drips off the spoon onto my shirt. Oh man. I shove the spoon back in my mouth as I try to rub the stain off my t-shirt. (Where is some tide-on-the-go when I need it?) It's pretty hard as my purse is hanging over my right arm and I'm holding the open carton of ice cream in my left hand.

"What is going on, Shanny?" Coen demands as he opens the door.

His expression is heart-breaking. It starts as a mix of bemusement and shock, which turns into pity. (Oh great. That is just what I wanted- pity from Conrad. Why did I come?)

"You look horrible," he says.

"Thanks," I say. "Can I come in?'

"Why do you want to come in?" he asks skeptically.

"I need love," I say shaking my head.

"What?" he laughs nervously.

"I need some quality Emperor time."

"Oh. Not getting enough love from the box of ice cream?" he asks back to his old self.

"No, I am not," I state articulately.

"Shanny," he says slowly, "are you- are you drunk?"

"Ice cream drunk," I say.

"What is it, Rum Raisin? Heavy on the rum?" He lifts up my arm to look at the carton. "Rocky Road? How apt. How poetic. *(How about letting me in your house? Why is he still standing in the doorway? Come on Coen.)* I didn't know Safeway sold this brand of ice cream."

"They don't. I wouldn't buy ice cream there if my life depended on it."

"What are you talking about Shanny?"

"I will not buy ice cream from a store that fired me!"

"You got fired? From Safeway?"

"I don't know. It's not like they said 'You're fired.' But does anyone say that? *(Besides Donald Trump?)* All I know is I definitely don't work there anymore. Okay? So, I am getting ice cream drunk. And I would like to see my dog."

"Who is it Coen?" comes a lilting voice from behind him.

"It's just Shanny."

Of course it's just Shanny.

"Oh. Hi Shanny," says Val. As usual, she looks ready to walk a Parisian catwalk.

"Hi Val," I say back. Could I have picked a better time to dress like this?

"Shanny is having a rough day. She needs some quality Emperor time."

"You need time with the beast?" she asks me without any understanding. Like I'm completely crazy for wanting to visit a dog. I guess some people just aren't dog people.

"Yes, I do," I say and push my spoon back into the ice cream.

"So, maybe we'll change our plans, hey Val? We'll go out to eat," he says apologetically. "We were going to order in and have a low key night at home," he says to me.

This is how they dress for a night in? No wonder I'm perpetually single. Maybe I should take notes.

He goes on, "But I think we'll head out and give you some space."

"Thanks," I say and take another bite of ice cream.

I follow them inside, feeling almost like a stranger in my best friend's house.

Coen and Val head into the kitchen to decide on their plans for the evening. I take off my shoes and hear that wonderful familiar sound of paws thundering towards me.

"Emperor!" I say. "Hey buddy!"

He is happy to see me and loves the ear scratching but he is digging his head into my purse. I gently pull his head out. "Hey! No, no, no, no, no. That is not for you." I reach in and pull out the squeeze bottle of chocolate sauce that I brought along. (There is never too much chocolate. But often there isn't enough so- boom!- chocolate sauce.) Emperor desperately tries to lick the top cap, but I manage to keep it out of reach.

I spend a few minutes scratching his back and talking to him before I finally get up to mosey into the living room. What will I watch tonight?

"Well, Shan," says Coen, "what are you going to watch while we're out?"

"I don't know."

"If you want to order some food or something, there are takeout menus and cash in the drawer. What am I saying? You know all that."

"Yes. I know that." (And I know what else is in that drawer.)

He sits next to me for a minute. He takes the spoon out my hand and tosses it into the ice cream. He grabs my hand and says, "Really Shan, things will be fine. You'll see. You didn't need that job anyway. You'll be on to something better in no time. Hasn't anything come from meeting with Chance Barley?"

"I still haven't met with him."

"Well, maybe something will still happen there. You just need to wait it out, you'll see."

"I'm ready to go Coen," Val calls as she puts in her hoop earrings in the front hall. (I wonder if he bought those for her.)

He smiles that smile at her then turns back to me. "Looks like she's ready. Time to go. Stay as long as you like, Shan. Just make sure that you lock the door when you leave. If you fall asleep, just make sure the television is off, k?"

"Sure. Thanks, Coen."

"I would tell you not to let Emperor on the couch but I know you do whenever I'm not here." (It's true. I do. I can't help it. He just looks so sad having to sit on the floor all alone.) "We'll see you tomorrow night at the party."

"You're coming to that?" I ask, surprised.

"Of course."

"Who invited you?"

"Your mom."

My mom. Of course. She would invite Coen to Connor and Meaghan's engagement party. And of course he would bring Val.

"Well, that's nice but I'm not sure if I'm going," I say.

"That's just the ice cream talking," says Coen with a knowing smile.

"Conrad, let's go," calls Val again.

"One second, Babe," he says. *(Who calls anyone Babe? What is she a baseball legend? Should I start calling her the Great Bambino?)* "Shanny, you're going tomorrow night. We'll see you then. Bye. Don't drink too much," he adds eyeing my melting Rocky Road.

"Bye, Coen," I say. "Bye, Val." I call after her.

A click. And the door is closed. And they are gone. And it is me and Emperor, alone at last. I call him and up he jumps onto the couch next to me. He nestles his head in my lap as I start channel surfing.

My stomach is not happy with me. Eugh. Why did I eat half a carton of ice cream?

Why can't I stop? Why am I holding the chocolate syrup in my hand ready to down it?

Oh man.

How did this become my life?

I wasn't being dramatic when I told Coen I may not be going tomorrow night. Yes, the night is for my brother and his new fiancé. Yes, it feels like I should be the good sister/daughter and show up and be cheerful and supportive. But I know the truth. The evening will become my mother's opportunity to play her favorite pass time- the "list all that Shanny doesn't have" game.

It's not like I need her to do it. I can fill in the list quite nicely on my own. Hey- I can even add things that she doesn't know about:

Shanny doesn't have all her bone marrow.

Shanny doesn't have any clue about Charlie.

Shanny doesn't have a job.

Shanny doesn't have the skills needed to work at Safeway.

Shanny doesn't have any friends at Safeway.

Shanny doesn't have the ability to walk through a parking lot unscathed.

Shanny doesn't have any prospects.

All of these things can be added to the long-standing list: Shanny doesn't have a husband; Shanny doesn't have a boyfriend; Shanny doesn't have a degree; Shanny doesn't have a career; Shanny doesn't have children; Shanny doesn't have a house; Shanny doesn't have a nice car; Shanny doesn't have any girl friends (Ryan doesn't really count); and Shanny doesn't have a father (I guess there's no one, but cancer, to blame for that really, but it's still true.)

Emperor looks at me thoughtfully, reminding me that Shanny also doesn't have a dog. "Well, you might not belong to me, but I love you," I say to him and scratch his ears.

I browse through the channel menu. Nothing really jumps out at me and I start to think that maybe I should rent a chick flick. I hardly ever watch those and I would never tell anyone I did. But as I think about which one I would rent, I become bored just thinking about how they're all about some sad single gal who has to make a change in her life.

Eugh. I don't want to have to make a change. I want a change to happen and make me. But maybe this is just not the place where things, changes, happen. Maybe I need to take a page out of so many chick flicks and go on some sort of soul-searching sojourn. But I don't have the money. Well, I could have it. No. Nope. Don't even think about it, Shanny! That money is not for a pleasure cruise. That money actually isn't even for me. I've got to get rid of it.

      Finally, something on the menu catches my eye and I flip the channel to watch the new Terminator movie. That's one thing I don't have that will cheer me up: Shanny doesn't have a homicidal robot after her.

Chapter 15

Shanny is… going with the flow.

I am at the party. Why am I at the party, you may ask. Because I am a weakling and I bend to the forced pressure of my family. Okay, maybe that is overdramatic. (No maybe- it is definitely overdramatic.) And to be honest, being here isn't the worst thing ever- there is good food. My mom is catering the event after all and she's pulled out the big guns. Another great thing about an engagement party? No wedding cake. Enter the chocolate fountain. So at least while I have no one to talk to and nothing to do, I can occupy myself by drowning cubed fruit in milk chocolate.

I woke up early this morning at Coen's. I was asleep on the couch with Emperor and a nice warm blanket that Coen must have draped over me after they came back last night. He brought me waffles and orange juice before he sent me home. He promised that today would be a better day. I almost believed him. But then I got home and spent the day procrastinating before I finally got ready for the party and dragged my behind to my mother's house.

When I congratulated Connor and Meaghan, Connor lectured me about how unnecessary it is to add chocolate to fruit. "Why can't you just be happy with nature's goodness?" he asked with his eyes rolling.

"Isn't chocolate a part of nature's goodness?" I ask. "In fact, I believe it's the goodest part of nature's goodness."

Meaghan winks at me behind Connor's back as he shakes his head in furtive disappointment. I'm sure I will see her stopping over at the chocolate fountain soon enough. I just give Connor a hug and head back to my seat on the alcove- none of the visitors have discovered it yet.

I sit there on my own, content to eat my fruit in peace.

I'm not on my own for long. Liam and Kim find their way over to me. There isn't enough space for all of us to sit but I scoot over so that at least Kim can sit next to me. Liam leans against the wall with cradling his cranberry drink in his hands. Kim raises her eyebrows purposefully at me (maybe it is a matter of nurture, she seems to have learned it from Liam) and I know exactly what she wants.

"Sure, help yourself," I say and hold my plate in front of her. She grabs a strawberry and a pineapple and wolfs them down. (She and I have more in common than I thought. Those are my two favorites too.) "Good, huh?"

"Yes. Good," she says.

"Can I have one of those?" asks Liam.

"Sure." He grabs three. I'm not trying to be a cow, but come on, Liam. If you want three, ask for three- not one. Now I'm going to look like a ravenous beast when I go back for seconds (Okay fine, thirds. Okay fine, fourths.)

"So. How are you feeling, Shanny?" Liam asks. "Have you recovered?"

I wave my leg slightly in the air. "Other than having to wear the walking cast, I'm pretty good."

"How much longer?" asks Kim.

"Not really sure. Probably a month at least." I answer.

"Not a great way to end the summer is it?" (Thanks for pointing that out Liam. I mean, my summer has just been stellar so far.)

I just sit there tight lipped. None of us say anything for a while. We are content to just people watch, having our own individual internal dialogues. I see Mom and some old guy laughing. I see Connor and Gavin and their girls. I see neighbors and family friends I've known since I was a little girl. I don't see anyone I consider a friend.

Then one of Mom's friends, Barb Underhill, sees me and waddles over.

"Shannon!' she says with a ridiculous patronizing smile. "How are you? We heard about your accident. How terrible!"

"Yeah, it-"

"But it must have been nice for you to have a break from your job at Safeway. How is that going by the way? Have you been promoted yet? Your mom probably would have told me if you were, right? So, you're what? A cashier? Well, that's nice."

Liam is looking at her with the same look I have.

"And have you finished your degree? You were going to, right? What was it in again? Art history? No wait- it was in philosophy wasn't it?"

I have to stop this. "Barb. Have you had any of this chocolate? You should. It's great. I'll go get you some if you like."

She looks at me as though I am the rudest girl ever born and bred.

That fake plastic grin, the doppelganger of a frown, spreads widely across her newly botoxed face. "I stay away from the sweets,

Shanny. Not a bad idea for you either. I may go and grab some of your mother's crudités though."

She turns on her heel and waddles away. Eugh- my mother's friends. Better no friends than those friends. I'm content to return to my solitary musings.

But then I have a feeling that Kim is watching me. I look back at her. She is watching me.

"You have a question or something?" I ask her.

Kim smiles sadly-ish at me. "You are angry person today."

"Today?" I ask.

"Yes. You are not usual Shanny. Usual, happy Shanny person."

I am honestly surprised by her words. "You think I'm a happy person?"

Kim's smile is no longer sad. "Yes. You, Shanny, get along with everyone. You are even nice to my parents. Not everyone is that." She grabs Liam's hand. "Just you and Liam. Most people get too mad to try to talk with them. But you- friendly, happy, nice."

This does not sound like me. Maybe she's mistaken me for someone else.

"She has a point, Shanny," Liam chimes in. "Maybe the accident knocked something around in your personality or in your brain or something."

Maybe someone has knocked your brain around, Liam. But really, do they think I'm normally nice? I have to change the subject.

"Who is that old guy hanging on Mom's every word?"

Liam looks surprised. "That's Chance Barley, Shanny. You've met him before."

"No I haven't." (And why is Chance Barley hanging around my mother?)

"He came to the hospital while you were in recovery."

"Was I awake?"

"I guess not, not when he got there. But Mom told him to wait around. I left right after he got there. It was kind of awkward being in the hospital with Mom and Chance and you lying there knocked out. I just assumed you'd wake up and meet him."

This is weird. "Nope. That never happened, Liam. I've never met Chance Barley. Only Charlie."

"You've met Charlie?"

"Yes. I told you that already."

"Charlie is nice. Very happy person," says Kim.

"He is, isn't he?" I reply.

"Yes. And handsome too."

Liam brings himself back into the discussion. "Anyway, Chance was there. He and Mom met and I guess she invited him here tonight."

We all watch them. They look strangely cozy. Mom just laughed and touched his arm. I have never seen that before. I am getting freaked out. Is my mom trying to be in her own movie- "How Muriel Got Her Groove Back?" Could she do this somewhere else please? People are trying to eat! (Okay maybe I'm still overreacting. But Kim said it, I am angry person today.)

My gaze is disrupted by the return of Barb 'the undertaker' Underhill.

"You were right, Shannon," she says. "These chocolate-dipped fruits are delicious."

"I'm glad."

"I meant to ask, Shannon, who are you here with? Where is your date? Your mother told me you were seeing someone."

"She told you that, huh?" What is my mother doing to me?

"Yes. I asked her why you were still single and she said that you wouldn't be for much longer."

"Maybe she thought you were asking about Connor, Mrs. Underhill. Shanny is free as can be." (Thank for that Liam. You really are so helpful.)

"Well, I guess being single is great if you are focusing on having a career."

I wonder who would be most shocked if I punched this lady in the face. What is it with old women? Do I send off some kind of chemical that makes them crazy rude to me? Maybe I really am unaware of my facial expressions.

"Yes," I say. "My career is very important to me. And I am getting married soon. And I'm moving to Sweden."

"Oh, Shannon, you're such a character. Don't you worry someday it will be your turn."

"Thanks, Barb," I say over enunciating.

"I know it must be hard seeing all your brothers getting on with their lives but-"

"Sorry to interrupt, but I just have to steal Shanny away."

Oh Coen. Sometimes I love you. He reaches past good old Barb and grabs my hand. He pulls me up and away from the one-woman firing squad. A few people stop to stare at us as we hurry through the crowd, him dragging me with my clunky walking cast. We're finally by ourselves, standing in front of the big bay window in the dining room.

"Well, what was that about?" he asks me with a boyish grin.

"You know, the usual. A concerned citizen warning me that I am on my way to living a fruitless life."

"Like you need a warning about that?"

I laugh because the way he says it is chummy. "I know right?"

"Has everyone been harassing you like this this evening?"

"Not all evening. But that's just because Mom is taking up everyone's time discussing wedding plans for Connor and Meaghan. She is sooo excited. As if it's her wedding. As if they have nothing to do with it."

"Maybe I could deflect some of the attention?"

"Oh? How so?"

"Well, Val and I have something to announce. We're-" (speak of the devil and she appears. That wasn't really fair. She's not the devil. If anything, she's just one of his minions. Or he does what she tells him to do. But probably not.)

"Have you told her?" she asks Coen as she leans close to him and kisses him on the cheek.

Come on, Shanny, sincere smile, sincere smile. You can do it. "Told me what?" I ask feigning sincere interest.

Coen grabs Val's hand as he tells me, "We are engaged. Shanny, we're getting married. Congratulate us."

She flashes the ring at me. Yep. It's the ring from the kitchen drawer.

"That's tacky. *(Hang on. What did I, what did I say? I didn't just say that, did I? I look at their faces. I did. I did say that. Fix it,*

Shanny fix it!) I don't mean the ring! You thought I meant the ring? No! No, no, no! The ring is beautiful- gorgeous. The ring is great. I just mean announcing the engagement. That would be a tacky thing to do at someone else's engagement party. I mean, I wouldn't mind it. I think it's great. Congratulations you two!" I give them both a quick hug, Coen second. "I just mean my mom wouldn't like it."

As if on cue, Mom comes towards me carrying a tray of mini goat cheese quiches. "What wouldn't I like Shannon?" she asks skeptically, as if she is predicting a number of things I must have done to ruin her party, as though it's a foregone conclusion that I did something.

"Nothing Mom. Don't worry about it." (Don't even worry about it.)

"Shannon, just tell me so I can fix whatever you did," she says tersely.

"Really, Muriel, Shanny hasn't done anything but give me some sage advice."

"Oh?" she asks. (I can read the thought bubble over her head that says "doubtful!")

"Yes. She just reminded me that your son's engagement party is not the best place for me to announce my own future bliss."

"Your own future..? Why, Conrad, are you getting married?"

"I am."

"Well, that is just fantastic! Congratulations! That is wonderful! This must be the lucky woman."

"Muriel, this is Val. Val, this is Muriel, Shanny's mom."

"Nice to meet you," she says politely.

"Well, let me see the ring," my mom asks like a giddy co-ed at a bible college.

I want to choke. I want to swallow like twelve of those quiches and just choke right now. But I hate quiche, so no way. Maybe I'll just choke on my feelings. They've just about made their way up through my throat anyway.

Mom keeps on and on with the questions. "When are you getting married?"

"We haven't officially set a date yet," says Val.

"But we're thinking next August," Coen says. "Maybe in Mexico."

My mom shakes her head. "I don't understand these destination weddings. All you young people jetting off to get married. That's what you're supposed to do after the wedding- on your honeymoon."

Coen smiles patiently, "Well, we both like Mexico but we already know where we're going on our honeymoon-"

Paris.

"Paris," they say at the same time.

C'est magnifique. Aren't quiches French? That would make my suicide even more poetic. More apt. Please let the smile still be pasted on my face. Please. Please.

"How wonderful," Mom says. "I've never been. Chance says it's beautiful. He told me he would take me the next time he goes."

Wait a minute. What?

"Mom," I begin.

She interrupts me. "Shanny. I can't believe you would tell Conrad and Val not to share their news with us. This is the perfect place to announce this. There is love all around!"

Is there? Is there really? Are you in love, Mom? Are you racing off to Mexico with some old man you met in my hospital room because you're in love? What is going on?

"Come with me," she says and she pulls them across the room up onto the little platform she had installed for Connor and Meaghan. How easily my brother and his own love lost the spotlight. (Not that either of them care. This party has always been about my mother. Everyone knows that.)

"Excuse me, everyone," she says. "I have to make an announcement. Excuse me. I'll just wait a moment while you all quiet down."

Oh no. I have that terrible 'I'm-going-to-sneeze' feeling I get whenever I'm about to cry. And my throat is closing. And the room is too hot. I've got to get out of here right now. Oww. I bump into the table as I try to hurry quietly to the front door. When was that table moved here? Why is it dark? Move out of my way, you idiot.

"Shanny- where are you-?"

No time to answer you, Liam. I run, pathetically, for the door. Where is my shoe? Where is your stupid shoe Shanny? And your stupid purse? I run to the hall closet- is that clapping I hear? - and grab my stuff. I slide my foot into the sandal and manage to stumble through the pile of shoes at the front door. Suddenly, I hear everyone laughing.

I pull the door open and hobble outside to my car. (I thank whatever power there is in the universe who kept anyone from blocking my car.)

Just start the engine, Shanny. It starts. I drive. Just a little farther, Shanny, come on. You just need a parking lot.

It just happens to be a McDonalds. What a perfect place. So apt. I pull into the parking lot. I keep my seat belt and the engine on. Luckily, it's dark enough that no one can see me through my windshield.

I finally allow myself to take a deep breath. The floodgates open. Why am I so pathetic? Come on, Shanny! This doesn't actually change anything. Nothing in your life is any different. Stop crying. Eugh. What was that sound? Come on. You haven't lost anything, I tell myself. And it's true. There is no tangible thing that I've lost. I haven't lost anything but possibilities- far flung possibilities that had no hope of becoming reality but somehow wormed their way into my heart's imagination, making me think- Eugh. How did I ever let myself think that he would...? How come I can't just root him out? Come on Shanny. But I can't. Somehow, no matter what comes along, nothing knocks him out of there. And I sit here waiting for something bigger, stronger to come along and get him out while I really hope he'll just wake up and see me.

Well, now I see it all. I really have been stupid. My only consolation is that maybe no one knows.

What am I going to do? I can't just stay here and cry about it. And when I say here, I don't just mean the McDonalds parking lot. I have got to get out of here- no matter what it takes.

Chapter 16

Shanny is... a mystery

Ryan Cooper-Kokozka- What does that mean Shanny?

Gavin Hardy- Is Ryan serious with that question?

Ryan Cooper-Kokozka- What do you mean Gavin?

"Now here is the number they want you to call now that you've taken the money," the teller says as he passes me the paper. "The company asks for a confirmation message. Now, anything else I can do for you?"

Yes. How about sell me back my soul.

I guess there's no turning back now. Fifteen thousand dollars in my bank account. Well, really fourteen thousand, five hundred dollars. I did take out some cold hard cash to carry in my pocket for expenses. I swear I sat in the parking lot at the bank for over an hour. (That's my new thing it seems- sitting in my car in parking lots feeling depressed.) But really, what else am I going to do? I'm trapped. This city, that I've loved since I was a little girl, has suddenly become claustrophobic, it's caving in on me and everyone's watching. I just don't think I can handle this.

"I'm fine, thanks," I tell the teller and stuff the receipts and the cash in my bag.

Next stop- Austen's Camera Shop. (I know- it is hard to believe that someone actually has a successful specialty store that exists in my price range.) I need some good advice though. I don't really know anything about cameras but if I'm going away, I need to capture the moments with something better than one of those twenty-four shots disposable things. (Does anyone still buy those?)

I found about this place from my (previous) manager Doug, the art history student. He told me once that it was the only shop with a soul left in the city- I assume he meant the only shop that deals in photography- there are plenty of other small, independent, soul-filled shops. (In fact there's a wonderful little book shoppe. Yes- a shoppe. I go there when I don't know which book I want; somehow they always know.) Anyway, he told me that Mike Austen is the man who knows everything about all things photographic.

After turning down the wrong street four or five times, I end up at the right place. Right away, I can tell it's fantastic. The images in the window are captivating. (Even though I can't really tell what half of them are meant to be. And even though I can't tell what it is exactly that makes them great, I can tell that they are great.) There is one huge black and white one, maybe of a zebra, that catches my eye and as I look closer I see the M. Austen signed in the corner. Inexplicably, I grin and shrug my shoulders and nod my head- he must know what he's doing.

A chime sounds as I enter the store. That's welcoming. Unfortunately, everything else in the store is not. Rows of lenses. Shelves filled with films and disks and bulbs. Racks of bags. Walls covered in frames of all shapes and sizes (and price points.) Help me. (I really hope no one in this place tries to swindle me- it's very likely I could get taken. I'm about to panic. I feel like a diabetic assigned to be the judge at a bake-off.) The only other customer in the store is paying for her purchase. She and the cashier are blathering on with their technical jargon that I just cannot understand. (I could do that. I could roll up into a grocery store- not Safeway- and start up a confab about scanners and codes and promoting membership cards and all that. Wouldn't that be just sooo cool?) Anyway, they finish up and she leaves the store with some kind of intimidating apparatus. (I think it's called a tripod?)

The older man at the register puts his receipts away and turns his attentions to me. He smiles. It is a nice genuine smile and it puts me at ease.

"What can I do for you, Miss?" (Aww, this time I actually like being called Miss. But now one else gets to say it.)

I am bluntly honest. "I don't know anything about taking pictures. I don't know anything about cameras or film or digital or any of that. But I'm going on a trip and I want to take pictures that are better than just snaps taken with someone's iPhone. I think a photo should say something, be something, capture something. I just don't know anything about how to go about accomplishing that."

"Are you finished?" he asks and pushes his glasses back up his nose.

"Yes."

"Good. Here we go," he says and the wonderful wizard of awesomeness spends an hour (an hour!) going over things with me. He answers questions I never would have thought to ask. He lets me play with different cameras. He asks me questions about myself and my interests before making suggestions. He doesn't overwhelm me. He is amazing. I feel like we're coming close to a digital decision when he asks the ultimate question.

"I should have asked earlier," he says, "but where are you going, Shanny?"

I'm stumped. A vacant look so thick and filmy passes over my eyes that I can feel it. I shrug limply.

"I'm just going somewhere."

He narrows in on me. "Going somewhere? You're escaping aren't you?"

I try to avoid answering so direct a question. Who does he think he is? "I am going on an adventure," I say.

"You are." he agrees. He nods and knowingly says, "You are going to Italy."

"Italy?" I ask. "Why am I going to Italy?"

"Shanny, you want to learn about art, about images? You go to Italy. You want to go on an adventure when you've never been anywhere before and don't really know how to travel? You go to Italy. You want to discover your soul? You go to Italy."

No wonder Doug loves this guy- they are both on team Italian Art.

"You really think that's where I should go?" (Should I admit part of me was wishing he would say, 'Go to Peru. You will find your true love.' Like he's some sort of human fortune cookie. Oh well. At least he didn't say go to

Paris, the city of love. I think if he did I would strangle myself- or him- with the strap on the camera bag I'm holding right now.)

"Yes. And this is the camera you will take," he says holding up a really nice Pentax number. As he rings up my reasonable purchases (he doesn't even try to up sell me on an overly huge SD card) he hands me a pen and a paper and insists that I jot down every place he lists as musts for my journeying. This man is now my Yoda, my Gandalf, my kinder, gentler Gordon Ramsey. Is it crazy that I want to give him a hug? We are both smiling as he hands me my camera and all its accompanying bits in my new camera bag. I notice an odd-looking machine on the counter behind him.

"What is that, Mike?" I ask.

He tells me it's a classic Rollei Rolleiflex.

"Huh."

"What is it, Shanny? Interested? It's not for sale. Even for someone as keen as you."

"No. I don't want to buy it. I recognize it. We have one in the basement somewhere. I should say that my mom keeps it in the basement. It belonged to my dad I think."

"Your father has a Rollei Rolleiflex?"

"Had. He's dead."

"Oh. I'm sorry."

"Mike, that camera is just sitting there in the basement, collecting dust. If I can convince Mom to let it go, and I don't think it will be hard to, I'll bring it to you. You can have it."

"Shanny, that's too generous. Those machines are worth a lot."

"They're worth a lot to people who care about them. I think this world is full of people who have valuable things that they don't value. Consider it done, Mike. When I come back, the camera will be yours."

We shake on it though he seems to still doubt me. I'll show him though. I'll be good to my word. I am going to follow through, all the way through, on something. I am.

Next stop- travel agent. In less than an hour, I've booked my flight, my hotels, and my tours. (Not one of those all-inclusive things- that would never do. I just like to be prepared. Jetting off tomorrow is out of character enough. I don't think I'd like any more uncertainty. Besides, aren't travel agents supposed to be able to help you if you get stuck somewhere? That might be good, especially since no one else is going to know where I've gone.)

It's shocking how easy it becomes to spend money when you have it in the bank. It's like you're not really spending anything, you're just changing the numbers in an electronic holding tank. (I try to ignore the feeling that this ease only exists because I didn't actually earn the money.) I have somehow managed to draw a flimsy kind of line. I've not bought any clothes or anything for my trip. (Why buy now when you can buy in Italy, though, right?)

I pack my suitcase pretty quickly. I haven't really got too much to take. I set my passport and my cash, credit cards, and all the rest of my stuff out on my dinky coffee table, the one with one leg shorter than the rest. I think about taking a couple of my scarves, I could try to fool people into thinking I belong in Europe, what with my Hermes scarf and all. But I decide not to and just leave them where they belong, hanging in the closet.

I look around and remind myself that this, this, is one of the advantages of being the perpetually single gal. I have no ties, no obligations. I can run of when I choose. No one is going to miss me or suffer for my absence. All I have to do is check my mail and make sure my bills are up to date before I leave for the month.

Most of my mail isn't even really meant for me. It's all flyers and promises of easy credit cards until I sift through and find two personal things.

The first is a cell phone bill. The second is a post card.

Huh?

Charlie sent me a post card.

Oh.

It has a picture of Macchu Picchu on it. Did Charlie go to Macchu Picchu?

According to his note, he did.

Dear Shanny,

I hope you get this before I leave Peru but I am cheap and sent it by slow snail mail so there is no guarantee. I am here, working hard, trying to live up to your example. I'm having a great time- the kids are amazing. And even though I don't speak Spanish, I find I'm able to get around alright. Macchu Picchu was breath-taking as I'm sure you can see from this ten cent post card.

Has my uncle called you yet? Are you busily working in his offices? Or are you running around doing good deeds? Maybe both? I'll see you soon Shanny. Take good care of the lemon tree. I'm planning on buying you a mango one next if I can afford one, if I still have a job when I get back. You were right, by the way, the kids have been following me around everywhere. (I think they like making fun of my soccer skills.)

Yours truly,

Charlie Barley.

First I wonder, is it legal to send mail with a false name? Then I am so thrilled that he thought of me. Then I wonder, should I write him back? (I flip the card- there is no return address.) Then my heart sinks.

Eugh. Charlie thinks so much of me. He thinks I'm some sort of good person who grows things. How did he get such a false and inflated impression of me? We've met less than six times. But hey, in that short time, I've seen how wonderful he is. What does he know about me? That I'm unemployed, that I'm accident-prone, that I like plants. And that I tried to do something selfless, something "good for the world," to use his words.

What would he think if he knew? If he knew that I sold out? How disappointed would he be? I'm sure he'd take back saying that I was his inspiration. (He did say that once, didn't he?)

But it's too late. Tickets have been bought and paid for. Camera has been loaded. Suitcase has been packed.

And now I wish I hadn't read that card. Maybe I could have read it after the trip and things wouldn't feel so tainted. I wouldn't feel so, so whatever it is that I feel. Is cheap the right word?

But I can't stay here. No twenty cent postcard can convince me to stay. No postcard is going to keep me warm at night, or feed me pasta, or drag me along on a crazy adventure, or help me discover my soul. If Charlie were here though- no never mind thinking about that.

I call the airport shuttle and book a ride for tomorrow morning.

I'll call Liam in the morning to let him know where I've gone. He can tell everyone else if he wants and that way Kim will know she's going to have to care for my orchid and my lemon tree (who am I kidding? Her orchid. Her lemon tree.) for about a month.

I climb into bed, my mind racing and as I lift my leg up I remember that I am wearing a walking cast. And I will have to keep wearing it as I try to navigate my way through ancient cobblestone streets. Oh, Shanny. When will you get a brain? I try to console myself; at least I'm not planning to walk along the Great Wall of China or to climb the heights of Macchu Picchu. This is not going to be a restful night. I try to think about anything other than engagement parties and engagement rings.

Chapter 17

Shanny is… on her way.

  Have you ever noticed, when you're sitting in the airport waiting for your connecting plane to arrive so the crew can clean it down and gas it up, that there are two kinds of people? There's the kind of people who eagerly look for other passengers in wait to talk to and socialize with- a layover friend. Then there's the type that wants to be left alone. This person intensely hovers over a book or magazine and wears their headphones in a deliberately conspicuous manner. (Oh- that reminds me! I've got to put in my headphones. I deliberately charged my iPod all night.) Can you guess which one of these people I am?

  So, here I sit, minding my own business, listening to a little Regina Spektor. The woman next to me is trying desperately to calm her baby while reading to her other little person. (I have no sense for knowing how old kids are. This girl looks like she could be anywhere from four to nine to me.) I wonder if I should help? But the prospect of offering seems so socially awkward I just keep my head in my magazine, Marie Claire of course, and casually nod my head as though I am really into the music.

Across from me there is a young-ish couple. I say young-ish because they are clearly older than me but they still seem pretty young- maybe in their early thirties. The girl is resting her head on the man's shoulder as he is rubbing her neck. They both look stressed and sad. It feels rude to look their way though they are straight across from me.

On my other side, a filthy nature boy is reclined and, I assume, way too comfortable for a public waiting place. His knees are bent, his feet up on the seat, almost on mine. He's breathing pretty loud and he's taking up three seats. Who does he think he is? I am going to give him five minutes. If he moves any closer to me after five minutes, I am going to say something. I am. I swear. I really am.

Five minutes pass and all is well.

I wish I could say that but that is not what happened.

The dude kicked me.

I mean he kicked me!

And everyone saw.

I had to do something. Boarding won't be for another forty-five minutes, providing the plane is on time, and there are no other available seats in this section. I can't just move and I can't just let it slide. What to do? What to do?

I push his feet.

I mean I <u>push</u> his feet.

And he lands face first.

On the floor.

And everyone saw.

I only meant to push his feet onto the floor so he wouldn't kick me again but I guess I don't know my own strength. (Or, which is more likely, I didn't anticipate how scrawny hippie granola nature boy was.)

"What the hell, Man?" he asks from where he is now face down on the ground.

I purse my lips and consider looking away. But everyone saw.

He looks at me insistently, "What the hell?"

I look back and forth at the people staring at me and this guy on the ground. It feels like an eternity but I'm willing to bet it was less than three seconds. I say the first thing that pops in my head, "You kicked me."

"I kicked you?"

"Yes. You kicked me."

"I kicked you?" (What's wrong with this guy? Why does he keep repeating me?)

"Everyone saw it." I sound much more defensive than I intend.

"No way, man. I did not kick you." (Is he stoned? Don't they screen for that in the security lines?)

I look around for support. He follows my eye line. The sad couple nods at him slowly.

"Man, I didn't know I kicked you."

"Yeah, okay. We've established that."

He is still sitting on the ground. Oddly enough, he looks more comfortable down there than he did spread out on the chairs. I continue by asking an obvious, to me anyway, question. "Are you going to get up?"

"Oh yeah, I guess so, Man." He climbs to his knees and shakes his head as if there's a bolt loose rattling around in there. "I guess I was sleeping."

"Yeah, I guess so."

Everyone goes back to their business. I open my magazine, about to pick up where I left off when suddenly his scrawny hand is on my magazine. What does he want?

"Well," he says, "aren't you going to make up for pushing me on the ground?"

Oh great. What is this about?

In the most innocuous, non-romantic voice I can muster (and that is pretty non-romantic) I ask, "What do you have in mind?"

"Why don't you buy some food?" he says and pats his belly. "I'm hungry. I think that fall made me hungry."

What? This guy is so full of it. But everyone's started watching me again. I don't care. I am not going to buy this guy dinner. I just don't do that. Maybe I can find some sort of compromise. I quickly look around the terminal. We're in LaGuardia. Surrounding us are a Krispy Kreme, a T.G.I. Friday's, a Prêt, and two Starbucks'. Bingo. That's it. I'll drop some dollars at the coffee bar.

"How about a smoothie? I'll buy you a smoothie," I offer. (I'm not really a fan of the caffeinated corporation that seems to have commandeered the globe, but I wonder whether hippie boy will be on board with this.

"Starbucks? It's a deal," he says. (Apparently, he is on board. Like any good, self-respecting granola boy he is a devotee of Starbucks.)

I shove my stuff back into my carry-on bag and follow him off to the order counter.

"So, what do you want?" I ask him looking at the hieroglyphics on the menu. I'm reminded why I never go to coffee shops. They make me feel stupid. What does half this stuff actually mean? How can a coffee be tall? Or short? Or grande? And what the heck does Venti mean? (Is it like twenty or something? And what does that have to do with a coffee cup?) "How about one of those Orange Mango smoothie things?" I suggest.

"No, I know what I want," says what's-his-name (what is his name?)

He proceeds to order some ridiculously elaborate drink that I could never duplicate even if I were tortured, even if the lives of everyone in this airport depended upon my ability to re-order his drink. (I picture myself in one of those "Saw" movies, locked in a room, my arm hacked off, promised to be released if only I could remember. But I just can't.)

Oh- order's done.

Hippie boy grabs his coffee and runs. I pay the bill. (I wonder- can I count this as a good deed? Even if I can, I guess I'll have to discount it because I have a check in the negative column after kicking him. The way I figure it, there are three columns: good deeds, bad deeds, and deeds done unto me. This little episode means there is a check in each column, so really they could all be stricken.)

I didn't even get a drink and now that I turn around, I see I don't have a seat anymore either.

So, I head to the gate and just stand there, waiting, until they finally announce boarding. That exciting, show-stopping event takes long enough and ends with me sitting on a dirty plane. The aisles and the space between seats seriously need vacuuming. The plane is full and I am squirreled away in my window seat (thank heavens for that at least.) We go through the safety demonstration business and we take off.

Sitting next to me on this filthy flight is a friendly Flemish girl. She has short blonde hair and it is clear that she is embarking upon a well-rehearsed pre-flight ritual. She puts some strange bag of flavored nuts (who brings nuts onto a plane? They give you roasted peanuts for Pete's sake) into the seat pocket in front of her. She pulls an orange iPod out of her carry-on bag and carefully unwinds the cord, unplugging the headphones and then plugging them into the radio jack in the arm.

Then, out of her bag she pulls two pens, two magazines, and two novels- one "The Catcher in the Rye" and the other, "Jurassic Park." Who is this girl? Maybe she found those books in a hostel?

"You need a book?" she asks. (Oops. She must have seen me watching her…)

"I just have my magazine," I say and flash the high gloss cover towards her.

"Magazines are not long enough for this flight." Okay Miss-Know-It-All.

"You've taken this flight before?"

"Of course. This may be my," she says then pauses and rolls her eyes as the numbers race through her brain, "my twenty-fifth time on this flight."

Holy. Who flies from New York to Rome twenty-five times? (Maybe she has some kind of intense long distance romance? Or maybe some strange visa situation? Or maybe she is an air marshal? That must be it- she empties her bag so that she can get to her gun quickly. No, no. An air marshal keeps the gun on their person, like in a holster or something. This girl just flies a lot.)

"Wow," I say. "You must really like Italy."

"Oh yeah, sure. I go there to do my good work." (Huh? Oh. She's some sort of evangelist doing her Good Work… but then why is she reading Catcher in the Rye? That book has foul language. And prostitutes!)

I do not ask a follow up question but she must get it a lot so she goes on to explain that she is a dental nurse. Her family moved to the States a few years ago without her. She visits them and then flies to Rome where she catches transportation and travels to Moldova whenever she can to assist with surgeries. I guess kids really do need braces everywhere…

"Well, that's great," I say.

"You are American?" she asks me.

"No. I'm from Canada," I say.

"Yes. Canada in America."

What?

"No. Just Canada."

"Yes. But Canada is part of America."

"No it isn't."

"You have the same president. Obama."

What? How can this girl be a nurse? Didn't she say her family lives in the States? Are you kidding me?

"We do not have a president in Canada. We have a Prime Minister."

"Yes. But he works for the president. For Obama."

(Shut up!)

"Nobody in Canada works for Obama. We are not America. Our country is bigger. Our hockey teams beat them in the Olympics. We have universal health care and bank regulations," I fish through my purse and pull out my wallet. "Look! We have our own money."

She looks at my five dollar bill.

"Yes," she says. "You have dollars. Just like America."

"Lots of countries have dollars. Us, the U.S., Australia, New Zealand…"

"You have the same money because you are the same. Canadian- American, the same."

I can't believe how ticked I am. "That is offensive. You wouldn't say that Australians and... *(and? Think Shanny! New Zealandans? No. Newzies? No! That's ridiculous. New Zealanders? I don't know. Ack! Come on...)* that Australians and, and people from New Zealand are the same."

"No. No," she agreed. "They are very different. Like the Dutch and the Belgians."

I'm done. As soon as they tell us we can, I put on my head phones and plan to keep to myself for the rest of the flight. She can keep her weird peanuts and ignorant ideas to herself. She wasn't wrong though, this magazine was not enough to read for the entire nine hour flight. And my iPod died. And the in-flight movie was bloody Harry Potter. (Nothing against Hogwarts or anything, just, a three hour movie about teenage wizards is not the best way to pass the time while you are stuck in a tiny seat with weird ignorant foreigners and food that tastes more like plastic than pasta. I cannot wait to land.)

Finally, with more bumps than my stomach cares to remember, we land and I am free from the worst flight I've ever been on. (So it's only been two. So what? Go hang out with Rembrandt girl if you have a problem with that. I mean Rembrandt the artist not Rembrandt the toothpaste. You can spend your time discussing how Canada and the U.S. are just two halves of the same nation.)

I wait in line amidst all the fabulous travelers feeling like hippie boy's twin sister. I can smell the travel B.O. all over me. Gross. Eventually, I get my bags and catch a taxi, ready for my first fabulous night in Rome.

I fall asleep in the taxi on my way to the airport, only to be rudely woken up by the impatient driver.

"Sorry, sorry," is all I can manage to say.

I look at my hotel. This place is a dump straight out of America-town. There is nothing adventurous or soul-stirring about it. I just want to cry. Why did I use a travel agent?

Chapter 18

Shanny is... fine. Don't worry about it.

Muriel Hardy- Shannon where are you? Why didn't you tell me you were going away???

Gavin Hardy- Yeah Shanny, where are you? Bring me something good back. Maybe something I can use for school?

Ryan Cooper-Kokozka- Bring me something too. Call me as soon as you get back. I have news. And Sam wants to talk to you.

Muriel Hardy- Who is Sam?

Ryan Cooper-Kokozka- Same is Brian's friend. He and Shanny went out once.

Muriel Hardy- They did? Why didn't she tell me about it?

Ryan Cooper-Kokozka- I guess Shanny likes to be mysterious.

Muriel Hardy- Well I don't get it. Why doesn't she call me?

Ryan Cooper-Kokozka- You know how she is. Anyway, how are you doing Muriel?

Muriel Hardy- I'm doing well thanks. It was nice to see you at the engagement party. Too bad you got there after Shannon left. Conrad was there too but I think you missed him too.

Ryan Cooper-Kokozka- Yeah. That's too bad. Brian and I have big news.

Muriel Hardy- Oh? What is it?

Gavin Hardy- Have you ladies ever heard of a phone? It's a great way to have a conversation. You can talk about whatever you want without everyone having to read updates every two seconds.

Muriel Hardy- That's a little rude Gavin. Ryan, what's your news?

Ryan Cooper-Kokozka- I'll let you know after I talk to Shanny.

Muriel Hardy- Who knows when that will be?

Muriel Hardy- Shanny! Call your mother! Where are you?

Chapter 19

Shanny is... honestly fine. Stop using my Facebook page as your discussion board.

Ryan Cooper-Kokozka- I'll stop when you call me. Are you secretly at home? Just ignoring all of us? What is going on?

Muriel Hardy- Shannon. Call me. We're all getting worried. Liam said we don't need to worry. Why does Liam know where you are and I don't??

    I have made a pledge to myself that I will not check my Facebook for the rest of my trip. But I've never been able to keep a pledge. (I've never stayed off chocolate for more than two days; I've never kept a journal for more than a week; I've never run a 10k race; and I've never done an entirely selfless act- I cashed the stupid cheque and jetted off didn't I?) So, who knows if I will this time or not?

    Rome is, well, it's Rome. The Coliseum was old and interesting. But I didn't find my soul walking on the arena sands where people fought and killed like desperate animals. (I didn't find Russell Crowe there either.) I didn't find my soul waiting in line for three and a half hours to get into Vatican City. I wasn't inspired watching the tourists stare up at the ceiling of the Sistine Chapel snapping photos in a compulsive frenzy- like they're worried they'll be asked to leave if they come up for air. (I'm not sure that Michelangelo had such a form of lighting in mind when he designed and painted the ceiling. Probably whoever paid him to paint it, didn't envision this flock of photographers either. Who was the patron anyway? Doug would know. Probably, Coen would know.)

I have eaten some great food in the three days I've been here. I know it's stereotypical and unimaginative but I'm on vacation and if I want to live on pizza and gelato, I will live on pizza and gelato.

It has been hard to hobble around with my cast so I've done a lot of sitting, which is fine.   I am on vacation.

I haven't bought any souvenirs yet- I'm not sure what I want to remember from this little jaunt. I wonder if I should buy anybody a gift. Maybe they would all be insulted if I don't. After all, most of them did bring me something while I was in the hospital.

Yesterday I spent most of my time in my hotel room. I had three showers. I couldn't decide what to wear. I ordered room service. I decide that today is not going to be a wasted day like that. I'm not going to feel sorry for myself on my last day in beautiful Roma. Mike sold me on this place and I'm going to find something wonderful about it before I drive north. (Well, technically I'm not driving- I'm taking a bus.

It's going to pick me up from the hotel early in the morning. I can't believe I'm taking a bus. I guess I'm just really tough or something. Even with the terrible memory of that old woman and her love of busses, I can still steel myself enough to get myself onto a bus. I am iron man- or woman- or something.)

There is only one decision that I have yet to make. To dress like a tourist who care or to dress like a tourist who couldn't care less? That is the decision. I really didn't pack enough. No matter what I wear, I won't look great but even I have limits where I no longer wear sweats or two day old t-shirts. So, I put on my favorite pair of jeans and a clean white t-shirt. I grab my sunglasses. (Ooh- maybe I could buy a fancy pair of Italian sunglasses- Gucci, or Versace, or some other brand that ends in an Italian vowel. I really don't know much about sunglasses but I do love them) I throw on my sandal (yes- a sandal) and my purse/day bag. (I had to get a bag big enough for my camera.)

Here is the day's plan: wander around aimlessly, taking photographs of anything and everything. I capture just about everything I see- architecture, bright clothes in shop windows, gorgeous old buildings, vespers, alley ways, signs, graffiti, people (if they look friendly. I think most of them feel sorry for me when they see my cast so they let me snap their photos.)

I end up down a road full of construction. They must be excavating. I guess in these old cities they can't build anything until they've dug around, ensuring that they're not building on top of some rare wonderful antiquity (like a dead emperor or a building that once housed some ancient philosopher or the first pizza oven.) There are lots of interesting things to take pictures of- crazy wires and such. I snap my pics and keep wandering until I come to a bench. This is good. My foot needs a break.

I think I'm across from a park- oh, nope. It's a school. I can tell this because the bell rings and out runs a bunch of little kids in uniforms. (Also, probably the sign in front says that it's a school.) The kids look pretty cute. They sound pretty cute. (Kids speaking another language in their little voices always sound smart and cute- that also usually applies to little kids speaking in different accents.)

A few of them start clapping and cheering as one of them runs up with a football (soccer ball.) Of course, my minds summersaults over the Atlantic to Peru. I wonder what Charlie is up to right now? Maybe he's running around in a place like this with his little students. I'm sure he's happy. Maybe he's planning a trek to some of Peru's sights other than Macchu Picchu. I take a minute to let my mind wander- what would we be doing if I was with him there?

What would we be doing if he was with me here? My thoughts are generally pleasant and G-rated. But then out of nowhere, I think what Coen and Val would be doing if they were in Rome right now and I want to puke.

The sound of the ball hitting the fence mercifully jostles me back to reality. I decide to haul my butt back to the hotel. It has been a long afternoon. I'll rest my foot and pick out a sweater to wear for dinner.

I have a nice, long nap with the fan whirring away- it is Rome in the summer after all. I get up, wash my face, put my jeans back on and grab a pink cardigan to wear over my white t-shirt. I take the old elevator down to the concierge's desk of my might-as-well-be-a - Motel 6 Italian hotel.

So, I have already eliminated a couple of things from off the docket for tonight. I will not be climbing the Spanish Steps with my boxy lump of a foot. (Even though I would like to go and see the house where John Keats died. Am I completely morbid? I'm not the only one. Why do people flock to places where famous people died? What is that about? We are a weird species.) The Spanish Steps are supposed to be totally beautiful but maybe I'll have the chance to check them out the next time I pop over to Italia.

The other escapade that is not to be is the staple visit to the Mouth of Truth. Why am I not going to test if the mouth will bite off my hand if I tell a lie? Well, first of all I have no one to lie to (does lying to myself count?) Second, the likelihood that I will find Gregory Peck waiting there for me is nil. (And who am I kidding? I am no Audrey Hepburn.) I do think for a minute it may be entertaining to go and watch the lineup of tourists waiting for their chance of a lifetime- to stick their hands in a hole just on the impossible chance the statue will be hungry and chomp down on their hands, tearing them off, forcing them to go on disability. (Maybe the settlement is how they plan to pay for their little Italian sojourn? What a bunch of lazy slugs. Who uses money from an injury to go on vacation?)

Well, what am I going to do?

I leave my lovely little dilapidated dwelling and try to hail a taxi to head off to the Mecca of Roman tourist activity- the Piazza Navona. Managing to get a taxi in this city is quite the feat. But I think I am subconsciously making my cast stick out, which in turn, makes the drivers and other seekers of relatively cheap transportation feel sorry for me. So it only takes a few minutes before I get a ride to the tourist hot spot. My driver drops me off and I give him a fair tip. I am actually pretty good at walking with this cast now and I maneuver my way through the thinning crowds to a good spot to sit and watch the happenings. (I am not sitting at a café. I don't care if I do have the cash; I refuse to pay the overblown prices for food and the pleasure of eating here. When I get hungry, I'll go somewhere else.)

I don't carry around a guidebook with me because, honestly, if I don't have someone to impress with my knowledge of fountains and dates and uses and sites and whatever, I don't really worry about facts. With my camera in hand, I'm just soaking in the atmosphere. The fountains are beautiful in the evening glow. I even like the one in the middle, with its ornate sculptured figures and then strange tall boxy pyramid thing (Oh- I just heard someone say it's called an obelisk) sticking out of the middle. It is strange to see a hulking block of stone jutting out of movement captured in marble. But there is something oddly exalting about this clunky block of stone thinning out and pointing to the sky.

It's pleasantly warm out even with the sun gone down and the varying smells of coffee and the expected Italian fare waft by. I'm suddenly reminded of my mother's kitchen on pasta Sunday and I feel a momentary pang of regret over not letting anyone know where I am. But that pang goes poof as I remember how nice it is to have breathing room, to have some private space. (Is it strange that I am feeling this in the middle of a crowd of tourists?)

Along the edges and at different ends of the piazza, there are musicians busking and artists sketching. I love this. This is what I wanted. Peace and atmosphere. I just have to try my best to avoid looking at the creepy mime who seems to be following me. Mimes are the most terrifying of all street performers. (Here is my theory why: they do not speak. Silence is the universal language of creepy. Not saying something and staring at innocent pedestrians while wearing all white make up and a tear drop drawn on your face is a bold declaration of issues. And why are they always fighting against the wind or trapped in a box? They're always in some sort of self-inflicted danger. Sir, you can free yourself! Just believe it and it will happen.)

I grab my camera, adjust the ISO setting and fiddle with the knobs just to experiment. I snap about a million pictures. Musicians playing, finely coiffed waiters waiting (or whatever their verb is), fat Texan tourists eating, people dancing. I experiment with framing objects, using the 9 zone grid thing Mike showed me. I snap photos of the ground, the sky, and the buildings that frame the long, skinny space. I actually think I'm getting pretty good.

I take a seat on one of the fountains and flip through my pictures. Some of them are badly lit but most of them are what I wanted them to be. I really like one of a sculpted dolphin in battle from one of the fountains. I also have to admit that some of the mime pictures are fabulously creepy. (Maybe one day when I have babies or nieces or nephews, I will frame one of them and put it up in their rooms.) Oh. I didn't even realize I took this one. It is as though I captured that stereotypical arty-ish painting that seems to be for sale in every pre-packaged home décor store. You know, the one with the woman in the red dress dancing with the man in the suit and the people holding the umbrellas? Well, my picture is missing the umbrellas but the fancy dressed people without shoes dancing are captured perfectly. I think I love it. I look at it for a while and then try to sift through the crowd to see if maybe the couple is still there. They aren't.

Suddenly, I'm not having such a great time. I turn off my camera and carefully replace it into my bag. I think I'll go back to the hotel now. I have to get up early for the bus tomorrow anyway.

Chapter 20

Shanny is...

Muriel Hardy- Shannon it's been a week!! Where are you??

I haven't checked my Facebook for five days. Pledge kept (for now.) Florence was fantastic. The Duomo, the markets, the Uffizi gallery, the stories about the Medici. To think I stood where the Bonfire of the Vanities happened is pretty wild. I think I could have spent a few more days there.

So why wasn't I happier?

I can tell why I'm unhappy now. Venice is the pits. Eugh. One day out and about was more than enough. But I booked this packaged tour thing and now I'm stuck here for two more days. The only thing I can think to do is buy a book in the hotel gift shop and sit in the lounge to read it. (At least this hotel is nicer than the last two, if it wasn't, that would have made staying in unbearable.) "Vaporetto 13" is the title I grabbed because clearly, the only thing better than being in Venice is being in Venice while reading a mystery novel set in Venice. Right?

Sitting across from me on a round leather chair is a nice looking old lady, but I'm not buying it- I've been fooled by nice old ladies before. (Fool me once…) She is reading a copy of Hello! magazine and every so often I can feel her look up at me with a pity-filled smile. (Oh man, I hate those smiles and I've seen enough of them in my time- usually at someone's wedding, usually accompanied by some sort of "you'll be next" or "someday you'll find him" promise- the repeated lecture geared towards the perpetually single gal.)

She abruptly folds the magazine in her lap and looks at me with her lips puckered to the side in deep thought.

I look up skeptically from my novel. (Not that I am really reading it- I'm on page four after twenty minutes. Come on, Shanny.) I must have raised my eyebrows or rolled my eyes or something because she grimaces at me with a Cheshire cat style grin.

"Alright, Miss," she says to me in her Scottish accent. "We need to talk."

Oh great. What is Grandmother MacWillow going to say to me?

She starts with a question, "What are you doing here?"

Okay. Broad question there, Granny. Do you mean here, as in on Earth? Are you going to sell me on your spiritual p.o.v.? Or do you mean here, as in in Venice? Or do you mean here as in in this hotel? You're going to have to be a little more specific.

"What are you doing inside the hotel on such a beautiful day here?" Yikes. Did she read my mind? Maybe she's a fortune teller. She just sits in foreign lobbies waiting for lonely girls to sit there silently begging for their fortune to be told. (What is she going to tell me? You will never find love. You will always be disappointed. You let yourself down.)

I smile politely. But I don't answer her.

"Dear, I know you understand English. I can see the book you're reading."

Hey! "I wasn't pretending not to understand you. I just don't feel like a chat, that's all."

"Why don't you feel like a chat?"

"Because this book is great. It's really got my attention. I mean, wow." Okay. That was so bad and unconvincing I feel myself closing the book and shaking it in my hand as I speak.

The old lady sort of giggles at me. "Well, I won't keep you then," she says.

"Besides, what are you doing here?" I ask more snidely than I had intended.

"I'm waiting for my husband to come back from the bank." (What a stupidly reasonable answer.)

"Well, that's nice."

"We're going on a gondola ride later."

"That's nice."

"Have you been on a gondola?"

"Yes." I went by myself last night- it was part of the package that I bought when I was under the misguided delusion that this trip would open windows to a world I'd never known. Oh, the gondola was a new experience alright- a whole new level of embarrassment. Me, alone in the gondola with a gondolier who wasn't wearing a striped shirt or one of those straw hats and who wouldn't sing, even when I offered a generous tip. (I couldn't believe I was asking him either, but I just couldn't stand the awkward quiet. And every other gondola seemed to have a singing driver.) It was so blissfully sweet to float along the canals seeing couples in love drifting along cuddled under a blanket. Really, it was just divine being the only solo rider on a romantic Italian evening.

"And how was it dear?"

"Terrible."

"Terrible?"

"Well, not terrible, but it wasn't the highlight of my life to sit in a slow boat watching sewage floating along next to me."

"That doesn't sound so bad."

"I could smell it too. And there were people everywhere making out in their gondolas."

"Making out?"

"They were probably all drunk," I offer as an explanation.

She looks at me as though I am speaking another language, but not a good language, like I was speaking something lame like Pig-Latin or Esperanto. I just shrug.

So, she tries another question. "What about Saint Marc Square? Have you been there?"

"Yes."

"And wasn't it lovely?"

"It was full of pigeons, dead pigeons, pigeons eating dead pigeons, tourists taking pictures of themselves basking in the crowd of pigeons, people eating McDonalds and feeding the fries to pigeons-"

"There are a lot of pigeons there. I see."

Have I made this awkward enough that she will go back to her magazine? Or watch the door waiting for her husband to come back?

"What about Ponte Rialto?" she asks. Apparently I have not.

"What? So I can buy a cheap knock off of a carnival masque or a mini gondola? Or be trampled by thousands of tourists complaining about the steps, which by the way are no piece of cake with my cast. Oh- or I could go at night and watch more people make out on the bridge. No thanks."

"Dear me, you're not very happy here are you?"

(What was your first clue?)

"I just hate Venice, that's all."

"No, no, that's not it. You don't hate Venice. You hate people," she says matter-of-factly.

"What?"

"You hate people, Dear. You hate them."

No I don't. "No, I don't."

"You do. It certainly sounds to me like you do."

Stop talking so casually! "Why would I hate people? I don't."

"You don't? Well, there's something you hate and it's rubbed off on poor little Venice."

"I didn't hate Florence."

"It's hard to hate Florence."

"The buildings are so beautiful. And the history- and the art."

"Yes, Dear. All the beautiful non-living things make Florence great for people who hate people."

This old woman has stopped me in my tracks. Who does she think she is to say these things to me? She doesn't know me. How dare she? I don't hate people. If I did, would I have friends? Would I have done a good deed that paid for this trip? Would I be ignoring everyone's messages? Would I be sitting here in Venice reading a book? Would I have taken so many pictures with my camera? (None of which have me in them.) If I hated people would I be crying right now? Wait a minute. Why am I crying? Oh no, Shanny, stop this. This is no quiet cry. People are stopping to watch. Stop. Hhhh. Stop! Try to breathe, you idiot. Come on.

But I can't stop. My stupid shoulders shake and I have emotional hiccups. All I can think to do is put my face in my hands, as though that somehow makes me invisible. This is not happening.

All of a sudden I feel dry and meaty, but somehow comforting, hands on my shoulders. The old lady pulls me up to my feet and gives my one of those crazy old grandma hugs- the kind you only see in overly emotional movies.

"There now, Dear. It'll be alright. You know the best thing about feelings?"

What? The best thing about feelings? Is she kidding? Here it comes.

"They aren't permanent." She taps me on the shoulder. "Have your little pity party. Be angry with whoever you're angry with, and then get over it. It does you no good to hate anybody. Just give yourself a little time and then move on."

She sees that I look skeptical, so she adds, "And if you really can't stand the person, just stay away from them."

"What if I can't?"

"Sure you can, Dear."

"No, I can't."

"Come on," she says and stands back to look me over. I have managed to calm down a fair bit. At least my chest isn't heaving and I can speak in coherent sentences.

"What I mean is, what if the person I can't stand is me?"

"Easy."

Oh really? Here it comes- maybe this is the self-esteem speech of a lifetime.

"You just go on and fix whatever it is that makes you feel that way."

What? That is terrible advice. What if I had a body image problem (which today, I don't at least)? Her advice could be an endorsement for an eating disorder. What if I was down because I was poor and her advice spurred me on to commit robbery? And what if I felt this way because I spent a bunch of money that wasn't mine and now I have to go home and make up for it?

"I'm leaving," I say.

"You're going out for the day?" she asked with a knowing smile.

"No. I'm going to Rome. I'm going to catch a flight. And I'm going home."

<u>Chapter 21</u>

Shanny is… home. But don't call me. I'll call you.

Muriel Hardy- When???

Ryan Cooper-Kokozka- When?

Gavin Hardy- What did you bring me?

Ryan Cooper-Kokozka- Ooh. Did you bring me something? And- call me! Big news.

     Can I guess what Ryan's news is? I haven't talked to her yet. I have a few things to sort out before I get back in touch with everyone. But I'm pretty sure I can deduce Ryan's news. Either they bought a new house, got a new dog, she got a new job, or she's pregnant. I think in a few days I will be in a better place to be genuinely excited for her.

     It happens to be Sunday so I decide to head over to Mom's early before dinner. Only about an hour, but maybe she needs help with something and it might be nice to talk to her and get the grilling over with before she has the full force of the family tag team behind her. It's a strange feeling to be nervous as I approach the door but oh well. (Maybe I am just trying too hard to block out what happened last time I was here. It was only just over two weeks ago. I have been away longer than that but never without letting her know I would be gone.)

Standing on the porch for a long minute, I take a deep breath. I knock. (I don't always knock, but I thought I would be polite. I might seem more penitent that way. Although I still have this raw nerve, a feeling like I shouldn't have to feel sorry.)

Mom answers the door. She's wearing her favorite apron, so I know she's in the middle of cooking a masterpiece. She's also wearing these really flashy turquoise earrings- strange, I've never seen those before. I would definitely remember- they're a little flashy compared to what she normally wears.

"Shannon," she says, more surprised than I'd expected.

"Hi Mom," I say back with an attempt at a smile. "I'm back. I thought I'd come by early to see if you need any help."

"Well, this is a surprise."

"I know."

"You should have called first."

Why isn't she letting me in? "Maybe. I just thought maybe we could talk face to face now since everyone will be here for dinner in a bit anyway."

"This is not really a good time for me to talk. I am busy in the kitchen."

Oh. "Alright, well, I also wanted to go down to the basement and look for something. So, I'll just stay out of your way until dinner."

I hear a sort of sizzling sound from the kitchen. Mom looks over her shoulder towards it.

"Do you need to check on that?" I ask.

"In a minute," she answers quickly. "What do you need to get down in the basement?"

A voice, a man's voice, calling from the kitchen stops my answer. "Muriel, I think the pot is boiling! I don't know what to do."

"Be right there," she calls. She turns back to me as though nothing just happened. "What did you need from the basement?"

"Umm, I wanted to get Dad's old box of cameras."

"That junk? I think I threw that away years ago."

"I'm pretty sure I saw it around Christmas time."

"No, I don't think you did."

"Can I just check?" Can you let me in?

Suddenly the face behind the voice appears. This guy is familiar. Do I know him?

"Oh, hi Shanny," he says, surprised, but with a smile on his face.

"Hi," I say just as my mom overlaps me.

"Shannon, you remember Mr. Barley?"

Oh.

"Actually, Shanny and I have never officially met. Nice to meet you Shanny," he says and extends his hand to me.

We shake. But hold on a second- why is he calling me Shanny? We're not friends. And why is he at my mother's house? On a Sunday? In the kitchen?

"Nice to meet you, Mr. Barley," I say.

"Please, Shanny, call me Chance."

My mother looks a little uncomfortable- like the cat caught with the canary- not in her mouth, but in her eyesight or something.

"Chance is here for Sunday supper," she says.

Thanks for the tip, Mom. I would never have guessed.

"Muriel," he says, "I think you need to check on the boiling pots in the kitchen. The water is ready for the lobster."

Lobster?

"You're making lobster for dinner tonight? You're breaking the bank and bucking the system huh?"

As my mom scurries off to the kitchen, she says, "Oh Shannon. You and your comments."

What? Lobster for seven, maybe nine, people? That's mucho bucks.

Okay- and cue the awkward silence.

Though it doesn't last long. Chance is a talker apparently.

"It's nice to see you up and about Shanny. You were in pretty bad shape from what I hear."

"Well, Mom always sees things at their worst," I say in response to his way too personal observation.

"It wasn't just your mom. Dr. Shoker was worried about you too."

"You talked to Dr. Shoker about me?"

"Oh- nothing intrusive or personal, Shanny. I stopped by the hospital to see how you were and met your mother. While we were speaking, Dr. Shoker came in and just expressed some concern about your recovery. Evidently, her worry was for nothing. You seem to be doing fine."

"I am fine. Thanks."

"You know, we were all quite impressed with your generosity."

"Who is we?" (I swear I'm trying not to be rude but this guy is just way too into my business.)

"Your mom, Liam, and I. And Charlie of course," he says with a casual smile.

"Well, that's nice. How is Charlie?" I ask.

"I assume he's well. I haven't heard from him."

"Oh?"

"Apparently that is a common trend with you young people- taking off and not letting anyone know how you're doing."

Is he lecturing me?

"Well, Charlie did tell you where he was going, right? He asked for the time off and all that?"

"Oh. Yes. He did do that alright."

"You didn't want him to go?" I can tell from his tone.

"This is a very busy time for our company. We're actually building a new tower. You knew that, I'm sure. But once Charlie gets an idea in his head…"

"It's hard to talk him out of it?" I venture.

"Well, not usually. Usually, I can convince him of the error of his ways. But this time he was surprisingly stubborn. He wouldn't even listen to Carol."

Oh no. Who is Carol? His girlfriend? His wife? Why didn't he tell me he was married? How could he? And why would he buy me a lemon tree? That's it. Okay, Shanny, try to keep your cool. You are jumping to crazy conclusions. Maybe.

"Well, I'm sure that there can't be too many objections for someone wanting to go on a humanitarian trip for a couple months," I say. "I mean, he's still young. When else will he have the chance to go? Maybe next time Carol can go with him?"

"Carol wouldn't be caught dead anywhere away from a five star hotel if she was down in South America."

Oh. So, Charlie's married to a high maintenance woman- probably fabulous and smart and with a good job. (Why do the guys I like always favor those kinds of girls, the kind who are the opposite of me?)

Where is my mom? This would be a good time for one of her trademark interruptions. How did I get stuck in this conversation? How do I get myself out of this?

"I've never stayed in a five star hotel," I say.

"Oh," Chance Barley says. "I thought you just jetted off on a five star vacation."

"Not exactly. *(Change topic now, Shanny.)* So, you don't know when Charlie is coming home?"

I'd like to know so I can give him a piece of my mind.

"No. No one knows for sure. He hasn't been in touch with anyone. *(Well, that's not entirely true.)* If his parents were alive, they would be worried."

His parents are dead? Oh. Poor Charlie. He never told me. Well, really when would he have had the chance?

"He is a grown man. He will be fine, I'm sure," I say pleasantly as I can.

"I'm sure he will."

"I just have to run down to the basement, if you'll excuse me."

"Do you need a hand?"

My mom comes back in wiping her hands on her apron. "Shanny can manage," she says. "Like I told you, Shanny, I don't think there's anything down there but you can check if you insist."

"Thanks, Mom. If you need any help with dinner, let me know."

"I actually won't need any help. It's just me and Chance today so you can go after you find the box if you need to."

"You mean no one's coming?" This is unprecedented.

"No. Gavin and Connor are at Meaghan's parents' house. I just decided to cancel Sunday dinner this week. I didn't know you'd be back," she adds pointedly.

"Alright," I say. "I'll just grab the box and head out of here. Enjoy your dinner."

I head to the basement and find the box exactly where I thought it would be. It's full of old cameras, lenses, etc. But there's nothing there that magically makes me feel like my father is in the box. I didn't realize that I was looking for that until it was so obviously not there. What was I hoping for? Some kind of note that he would have left in the box from beyond? Like- **"Dear Shanny, I knew some day you would look through this box and that you would love photography just like I do. I love you, little girl. -Dad."** What a childish thought.

I haul the box of goodies upstairs and out to my car without even a goodbye to my mom and her, her what? Her gentleman caller? Her dinner guest? Her boyfriend? No, no way. But why else is he here? For lobster? The world has become topsy-turvy. Since when does my mom pick up guys? Or maybe he pursued her. She must have looked pretty stellar compared to me laid up there in the hospital bed. Maybe reading that stupid self-help book actually worked for her.

I try to change my train of thought as I carefully place the box in my old beater car. I don't need to think about my mom being on a date or about Charlie being married. Hold on. Charlie does not wear a wedding ring. (As every good PSG does, I checked for the wedding ring.) But then who is Carol? His girlfriend? Or maybe his sister? Yes- that has to be it. I mean, that has to be it. Charlie would never be two-faced. How could someone so thoughtful who did such lovely things for me, me- not some vavavavoom chick- how could he be sketchy? He couldn't. He sent me a postcard. I wonder if there's a way I can send something to him?

I'll have to examine that postcard for any clues. Or maybe I could figure out which organization he's with? I consider my cleverness for figuring this all out as I pull out of the cul-de-sac and drive myself to Liam's. I just need to talk to him quickly before I head back to my apartment and relax for the night with a frozen pizza. (Do I have a frozen pizza in my freezer? Maybe I'll have to have a tuna sandwich or a salad or something. My fridge is stocked from yesterday's trip to non-Safeway, but I wasn't planning on making my own Sunday dinner. I haven't done that in years, that I can remember.)

Liam's house is only a ten minute drive. When I get there, he and Kim are out in the front yard, busying themselves with all things to do with yard and lawn maintenance.

"Shanny!" he calls and turns off his weed-whacker. "I was wondering when you would come and see us."

"Hi Liam. Hi Kim. How are you?"

"I am well, thank you, Shanny," Kim answers as she is bent over weeding around her floral bushes.

"What's up" Liam asks me as he comes near and takes off his gardening gloves. (I can't believe he wears floral print gardening gloves. What a girl! They must be Kim's.)

"I just came from Mom's house."

"Oh." (Aha! So he does know something!)

"What is going on there? Why is Chance Barley having dinner with our mother?"

"Did you talk to him?"

"Yes."

"Oh. Shanny are you mad?" As he asks this, Kim comes and stands next to him looking a mix of embarrassed and hopeful.

"Mad about what?"

"About the job thing?"

"What job thing?"

They exchange looks.

"Guys, can you just tell me what's going on?"

"Chance gave Kim the job that they had in mind for you," Liam says as Kim winces. (What does she think- I'm going to smack her or something?)

"How did that happen?" I ask.

"He met her at the engagement party, they got to talking, Mom told him that Kim did all the flowers for the party, and he offered her to job. Sorry, Shanny."

"Sorry, Shanny," Kim echoes.

"Sorry for what? I think that's great. Kim you should have a job like that, doing floral arrangements and whatever. If you want it, that is. I'm fine."

They both smile at me, relieved that I didn't turn into that little girl from 'The Exorcist' or something even more frightening. (Do people think I'm mental or something?)

Liam pats me on the shoulder. "But you do still need a job now, don't you Shanny?"

"Yes. But I'll find one. Don't worry about me."

"Of course, I worry about you, you crazy jetsetter. How was Italy by the way?"

"Italy was illuminating. That's all I really want to say about it."

"Okay, so why did you stop here? Not just to talk about Mom and her new friend…*(Do not say friend with benefits, do not say friend with benefits.)*…the business man."

(Phew.)

"No. Of course not, though I'm still weirded out by that whole thing. But I came to ask you about the message you left on my machine. Something about needing to talk to me about insurance."

"Oh, yeah. Come and sit down for a minute."

We go and sit on their porch swing, which is quite a perfect thing to do on a Sunday afternoon.

"I called the insurance corporation about your accident. And then I called a lawyer. You're entitled to a fair compensation, Shanny."

I am?

"What does that mean, 'fair'?" I ask.

"You know, based on precedent, able to cover your fees, plus more for the future."

(Like maybe five thousand dollars? Enough to make up for my un-entitled splurge?)

"Okay. Well, what do I do?"

"I'll book an appointment and we'll go in to see the adjuster this week."

"The sooner the better," I say.

"Sure, Shanny."

"Thanks Liam. Really. This is great," I say and get up to go home.

"I'll call you first thing in the morning," he says.

"Sounds great. Enjoy your Sunday dinner."

"You too," he says and closes the car door for me.

I roll the window down and wave goodbye as I back up their long gravel driveway.

So, now I have a few things to sort out. One, finding a way to send Charlie a letter; two, getting a fair deal with my settlement; three, finding a decent job. Once those things are sorted out, I'll be able to move on and do what I really need to do. I've got to give that money back.

Chapter 22

Shanny is… on the hunt for work.

I am. I do really need to find a job. But first I have to visit Mike at his shop and fulfill a little guarantee.

"Shanny!" he says happily as I come into the store. (I can't decide what I like more- the little bell that chimes when I open the door, or the friendly sound of my name being called.) The shop is almost deserted. (How does Mike manage to stay in business?)

"Hi Mike."

"You're back already. How was Italy?"

"Do you want the honest answer or the what-I-tell-everyone answer?"

He grimaces. "So, not the soul-stirring quest I promised?"

"Afraid not."

He clicks his tongue just before he says, "I'm sorry it wasn't what you'd hoped."

"Well, I don't know if I'd say that. I mean, it was no "Roman Holiday" but I got some things figured out and that is worth a lot to me. I don't think I would have managed to do that if I had stayed here, or gone somewhere else. I'm definitely not here to chew you out, if that's what you were worried about."

"Wasn't worried about that. You are not that kind of girl, I think, Shanny. You are to gracious."

(Oh- I love that. No one has ever called me gracious before, that I know of.)

"Well," I say in my most gracious voice, "in the spirit of generosity, I have brought you a gift. Well, one gift-ish thing, and one box of real gifts. Which would you like first?"

"Which one will take longer?" he says with his eyebrows raised high above his glasses in curiosity. (What a great question.)

"The gift-ish thing will take longer I think."

"Then give me the good stuff."

"Alright." I heave my big canvas save-the-earth-by-not-using-plastic-bags bag onto the counter. "Here you go. All for you."

I might die from delight as I watch Mike delicately take each old camera, pieces, lenses, etc. out of the bag. This is better than I had hoped. I am a genius sometimes, I really am. After a few minutes of almost silently picking through the objects, Mike stops and shakes his head.

"Shanny, you can't just give me all of this," he says quietly. (But I can tell what he really means is- thank you, please don't take it away.)

"Of course, I can. My mother was going to throw it away." (He looks at me in shock at such a blasphemous prospect.) "She thought she already did actually. So in a way, you are rescuing these things."

"But don't you want them?"

"I want to give them to you. So, I am."

"Thank you."

"You are welcome, Sir."

He carefully puts the pieces, including the intact Rollei Rolleiflex, onto the shelf behind him. "I'll put all those pieces away later," he says happily. "Now, what is the sort of gift thing that you have brought?"

I pull out my camera and my USB cord. "I just thought if you had time, I might show you the photos that I took on my trip. I'm sure a lot of them are junk, but some are pretty good, I think, anyway."

"I would love to look at your pictures," Mike says as he plugs the cord into his computer and my camera.

We spend quite a bit of time, picking through my images and Mike is kind enough to give me positive and helpful critiques. Some of the pictures are just laughable and we shake our heads. (I have enough humility that I can take every point with a student' view.) I have to say that every compliment makes me really proud. Mike especially loves the photographs that I took at the Piazza Navona. He also, for some reason beyond me, likes my Venetian pigeon pictures.

As we take a second look at a few of the better images, the doorbell chimes and in comes, of all people, Doug, former manager, only firer, Doug.

Mike greets him as warmly as he greeted me. "Doug, come and look at these pictures. I really think you'll get a kick out of them."

Doug approaches as Mike continues explaining. "Shanny here just got back from Italy and is displaying her beautiful, or should I say belissima, images for us."

"Mike, you should never say belissima," says Doug. "Hi Shanny," he adds as he turns the screen. "So, you went on a trip?"

"I did," I say as I move aside so he can have a better view and pick my work apart to death in his PhD way.

To my surprise, Doug is super positive. He and Mike talk about things (artist's techniques, terms, etc.) that I don't understand, but it all seems pretty positive. After a few minutes, Doug says to me, "Shanny, I'm really surprised. But I have to say, your work is great."

My work? I never thought I would do something that I would call my "work." Cool.

"Thanks Doug."

"I mean it. Have you thought of entering any contests?"

(My vacant look is obviously an answer to the negative.)

"Really. Some of these could make amazing prints."

"Well, thanks, Doug. But I don't really know anything about that stuff."

"I do. Listen Shanny, I feel pretty bad about the way you left Safeway, and I'd like to make up for it. So I will send some of these prints in if you'll let me."

"I don't want you to do anything for me out of pity. If the pictures aren't good enough and you're just being nice, I don't think you should waste your time. Or mine."

"He's not just being nice, Shanny," says Mike. "These pictures are first rate. Well, some of them. Not the ones of the sky or the ones of the architecture- I think you have a lot to learn about that sort of photography."

"Definitely," Doug agrees.

"But you capture people in a really interesting, unique way." (Maybe I have a gift for capturing images of what I hate. According to some, I hate people. But they're wrong. Maybe these pictures are proof that I have faith in my fellow men and that I have a joie-de-vivre deep down in my soul.)

"Thanks, guys," I say.

"We're going to help you out," says Mike. "In return for your generous gift to me, and because of Doug's guilt, and our joint belief in you, we will arrange for some of your work to be printed and sent to some art house and magazine competitions. No promises of what will happen. But we'll see. Alright?"

"Sure," I say. (Why not?) "I'm game."

"Good," they both say.

Mike gets to work uploading pictures onto his computer in a folder called "The Great Shanny." (How ridiculous.) Doug asks me to write down some information that they'll need about the photographs and me. (Things like address, dates, times, full name, camera type, etc.) Then Mike and Doug chat about which pictures are the strongest. (They both love the pics of the creepy mime- go figure.)

When Mike has finished with the upload, he unplugs my camera and puts everything carefully back into the case. Then he gives me a hug and orders me to come back to the store in a week. I agree without hesitating, say farewell to Doug and head for my car. This has been such a positive morning. I just feel myself beaming. Hopefully the happy love fest will continue this afternoon as Liam and I meet with the insurance adjuster.

Catherine Sterling is perhaps the most severe woman I've ever met. Barb Underhill is a roll-over, kind and generous pussy cat compared to this woman. And the fact is, if it wasn't totally messed up, I think Liam may have picked up her name plate off her desk and hit her over the head with it. (I have to admit, it was slightly thrilling to see my calm, responsible brother lose his cool. It was kind of devilishly wonderful to be the level-headed Hardy for once.)

I think Liam's protective side came out. The more she questioned me with her suspicions, the more he defended me. I had to remind him a couple of times that he hadn't actually been there and didn't actually witness the accident. His response was the same each time. "I saw you in that hospital bed, Shanny," he would say, "and I will never forget the sight of you lying there. You could have died."

Catherine would try to calm the situation but her questions pushed Liam over the edge.

With her overly -plucked thin eyebrows raised, she brought up the bone marrow donation. "I see here that you felt well enough to undergo a surgical procedure. Do I take that to mean that your injuries were not as severe as it has perhaps been suggested?"

"You do no such thing," Liam said angrily. "You can't use Shanny's generosity to penalize her."

And so on, and so on. That was how the meeting generally went. I had to put an end to it somehow. So I asked what they were offering. Catherine told me the settlement offer was three thousand dollars based on suffering and necessary physical rehabilitation.

I swear Liam's jaw literally dropped to the floor. I thought it may shatter but it stayed in place as he shook his head defiantly. (I wondered if he's protective or just greedy.) Anyway, eventually I managed to negotiate between the two of them, on my own, and I wound up with a settlement cheque of forty-five hundred dollars. Way to go Shanny! I am really proud of myself. I knew I was good at negotiating and mediating and all that. I got a good amount of money (totally fair I feel) and I kept the other two from hurting each other (or me in the crossfire.)

I don't think Liam felt quite as exultant as I did but he was happy that I stood up for myself. The cheque was cut and presented to me within a half an hour.

Now we're in Liam's car heading home. He is listening to some light music station. An old U2 song, "The Sweetest Thing" I think it's called, is playing.

Charlie… sigh…

"What was that, Shanny?"

Oh. Shoot. Was that out loud? (What can I say? What sounds like Charlie? Barley- no, been there, done that. Farley- why would I say that? Carley- do I even know a Carley? Gnarly- what am I a surfer or an old woman with crippled hands? To heck with it.)

"Nothing. I didn't say anything," I say.

"Alright," says Liam. "What are you going to do with your millions?"

"I know exactly what I'm going to do with the money," I say.

"Is this a secret, like your little Italian getaway or can you tell me?"

(Is it just me or does he sound kind of annoyed? Why should he be irritated? I told him where I went after all. Maybe he's just sore that I didn't let him throw down with the insurance adjuster. Maybe his plan was to get injured and then have a claim of his own? No that's ridiculous. Isn't it?)

"It's not a secret," I say. "I'm going to tell you. Eventually. I just have to earn another chunk of money before I can do what I'm planning. I'll tell you as soon as I do it."

I can see the wheels churning in his mind. He's thinking about all of the things I could possibly do with fifty-five hundred-ish dollars. He doesn't know that my plan involves quite a bit more than that.

We drive in relative quiet until he's just about to drop me at my apartment. I've got to ask him a question.

"Hey, Liam."

"Yes, Shanny?"

"You know Charlie?"

"Yes." (Did he smile a little?)

"Any idea which organization he went down to Peru with?"

"Why? You thinking of going down there to volunteer? That's what you're going to do with your money? Or you want to make a donation to them?"

"I just thought maybe I would send Charlie a letter. He was really nice to me before he left."

"I know. He gave you that lemon tree and everything."

"Yes, he did. So, do you know who he went with?"

"Sorry, Shanny, I don't. I don't think anyone at our office or even his uncle or Carol knows exactly where he is or who he's with."

"It's weird that he didn't tell anyone. I at least told you. He could have told his sister."

"His sister?"

"Carol."

"Carol isn't his sister." (The way Liam says that makes me want to smack him. He said 'isn't' and 'sister' like they were locker room words or something. Okay I get it. I get it now. They have a very non-sibling relationship.)

"Oh." (Come on Shanny, don't look so disappointed. Come on!)

We're here. Liam pulls over and I unbuckle.

"Shanny, just ask what you want to ask."

Fine. "Who is Carol?"

"Carol is his ex. Girlfriend, not wife. She just so happens to work in Chance's office, in the same department as Charlie. They broke up about six months ago."

"Oh."

"He was kind of a wreck."

"Oh."

"He's a nice guy. I hated seeing him like that."

"Yeah. I bet." (And now a whole new can of questions pops open.)

"I'll see you, Shanny," he says as I open the door.

I climb out of the car as I say good bye, completely unsatisfied by the abrupt end of the conversation. I have lots to do still. I need to track down Charlie. I need to cash this cheque. And I really need to find a job. I've decided to make a goal. It is Wednesday. Within one week I'm going to find a job. (And not at Safeway, not that they would hire me anyway but I'm going to act as though it's due to my standards, not theirs.)

Chapter 23

Shanny is… on the hunt for work. Still.

It's Monday. I still have two days to go. So far my search has not paid off. (But if I'm being honest, I haven't really tried very hard. I spent two days working on my resumé and looking through want ads, then writing cover letters. I think I've dropped off about six resumés.) I am determined to do more, to be better, but at a leisurely I-still-have-a-brokenish-foot pace. (My foot is no longer really a barrier to me though. Once you've traveled with a bum foot and hobbled along the streets of Rome, I figure navigating pavement and cement sidewalks is not so bad.)

I've just had lunch and I'm going to continue my scouting work, but first I've decided to swing by my old hang-out (and by the way, why is it called a hang out? Who's hanging? And it's usually inside, right?) So, I'm off to Mike's photo shop.

As I park and get out of my car, my phone buzzes- I have a message. (I wish I could get my phone to make a noise other than that is-there-a-monster-fly-around buzz, but I'm not going to pay good money (and yes, now I know there is good money and bad money) for a digital tune that will get just as annoying as the buzz in no time at all.

It's Coen. Huh. I haven't talked to him since I got home. Well, really, I haven't talked to him since the engagement party for Connor that became an engagement party for him and va-va-va-Val. I'm not sure I want to check this message. Will it be an angry chance for him to berate me over the phone or is it some sort of exultant invite to some celebration of their love? Turns out it's neither.

-Shanny, are you home? Are you okay? (That's what he texts me after two weeks being absent. I don't know how to feel about it but for some reason it irritates me.)

I hit the button to reply but I draw a blank. What do I say? I must look like an idiot, standing here, leaning against my car for so long, staring at my phone like some kind of weird street performer. (Oh no- at least I'm not wearing a striped shirt and won't be mistaken as a mime.) Snap out of it Shanny. The phone buzzes again.

-Where did you go? Call me okay? And make sure you're free three Fridays from now.

Is he getting married in three weeks? Why are all these people rushing into marriage? What happened to the weddings that take more than a year to plan? Come on people, be extravagant. Let things percolate. I mean, can you even get a dress made in two months? You cannot. I have watched enough episodes of "Say Yes to the Dress" to know that unless you are buying off the rack, you need at least six months. Val doesn't strike me as an "off the rack" type. So, why the rush? (Oh man, I've got to stop my mind from racing with all the possible explanations.) Okay, Shanny, just put the phone away and go into Mike's shop, your little refuge of late.

No such luck. Another buzz. I have to check it.

-Four Fridays from now. Engagement Party. 7 o'clock. My house. Hope you'll be there.

And another one.

-Where are you?

Conrad has never sent me so many texts in a row without some sort of reply in between. He seems really needy all of a sudden. Almost like Ryan. (He would be furious if I said that to his face.)

I debate texting him something like "I'll call you later," but then he might call me right then and there. I'll just get back to him later.

Huh. There was a time I would never even think of waiting to reply to a message from Coen. He is my best friend, after all. Maybe I've figured things out. I think I've realized that a text message is not a gesture of secret love. I mean, obviously it isn't. He has never thought about me that way. He would have done something, something that doesn't involve getting engaged to someone who is almost the opposite of me. So why am I so messed up about this? Just let it go. Why can't I just be happy for my friend? My friend. Eugh. Come on Shanny, move on. But it's like there's some sort of deep rooted feeling, like my affection for him got all confused and tangled up and the less likely it is that anything will happen, the tighter those roots dig in. Maybe I should just start listing all of the- whoa.

> Wait a minute.

> Hold the phone.

> Hang on.

> No way.

Is that my picture in Mike's window? Not a picture of me- a picture I took. No, not a picture I took- four pictures I took. They look, well, honestly, they look amazing. The smallest one is and 8x10- that size I recognize. But the other three are bigger (I don't even know what sizes they are.) And they're all framed, beautifully framed, expensively (I would bet) framed. In the corners of each, there are typed tags with my name on them. "Image by Shanny Hardy." And it says "Enquire within" and has Mike's shop's phone number. What is going on?

I run (well as much as I can with my gimp foot) into the shop. Abruptly I stop. There are a few customers in line so I don't just yell out to Mike, as much as I want to (and I really, really want to.) Instead, I stand near the rack of black and white arty postcards, pretending to peruse them intensely. Wait. Why pretend? I'll buy Charlie a postcard. I grab one that catches my eye, it's a picture of a cat hanging on to a branch and it says, "Hang in There Baby." Just kidding. I would never buy that and I don't think Mike would have such a lame cliché in his shop.

The postcard I pick up is a moody night time shot of a woman standing in the distance on an old worn down bridge. What does this have to do with Charlie or me and Charlie? Nada. Zip. (Shouldn't zip mean the opposite of nothing? It's such a peppy word after all. It is a word with zip. Hold on. I think I've just discovered a contranym!) Anyway, I just love the image. It's haunting and kind of sad, although Charlie is neither of those things. Maybe I am, today anyway. I flip it over to the back- of course Mike took the picture. This guy works so hard and puts himself out there. What is he doing putting me out there? In his shop window?

I wait in line, trying to hide from Mike so he won't see me 'til it's my turn to pay. It's not hard to hide from him; he's so focused on helping the current customer.

Finally, I get to the front and Mike beams. "Welcome back, Shanny! I can guess your question."

"I bet. What's going on here, Mike?"

"I decided to take my favorites of your pictures and put them in the window and see if any magic happens."

"That's so crazy. But really so nice, Mike."

"I know. I picked what I thought were your best ones."

"Well, if that's the case, why didn't you put the mime picture up?"

"I did." (Why is he smiling like that?)

"What, someone asked you take it down because it was scaring small children?"

"Nope." (Well what then?)

Mike opens the cash register and pulls out an envelope. "For you," he says.

(I've had enough of secret envelopes to last me a lifetime. I'm not James Bond. I'm not presenting at the Oscars.)

I take the letter skeptically. "What is it?"

"Congratulations, Shanny Hardy," he says with his great old man grin. "You are officially a paid artist."

"What?" Now I eagerly open the envelope. "Mike, there's one hundred and fifty-five dollars in here."

"I know. I deducted the cost of the print and the matting and the frame etc. The rest is all yours."

"Someone bought my photograph?"

Now he's laughing at me. "Yes."

"Why?"

"Probably to display it somewhere Shanny. They wouldn't spend that much to destroy it."

"Why would they want a picture of a mime?"

"Would you stop questioning everything Shanny? It was a fantastic image. Someone appreciated it and purchased it. That's good. You don't need to worry about it."

(I have this feeling like Mike's advice applies to more than my disbelief about my photograph.)

"I guess I'm just really surprised. I'm not really sure why you did all this." I say and gesture to the front window where my images of pigeons, and musicians, and dancers, and a lit alleyway are proudly displayed.

"You put good things out; good things come back to you. Karma."

"I've never really thought I had good Karma."

"Well, you do. So says I."

"Alright, Mike, thanks." A thought occurs. "Do you have the name of who bought the picture?"

"No, I didn't keep it."

"I'm just wondering if somehow somebody I know came in and bought it. But I don't think anyone knows about my pictures."

"Shanny! Someone who didn't know you bought your picture. It wasn't some generous pity deed. In fact, the buyer is considering coming back for the picture of the pigeons."

I shake my head but I can't stop smiling. "Thanks, Mike." I smile even wider as I realize I can put the money in my buy-back-my-good-karma fund. Oh man! This is great. "How long are you going to leave my pictures up? Is there a time limit?"

"Of course there is. If they don't sell in two weeks, I take them down and replace them with other prints. But I think you'll do fine. I only put them up yesterday."

I just can't stop smiling. I wasn't wrong-I am naturally good at something. That's kind of a miracle.

Mike finishes ringing in the post card. I pay for it with the five dollar bill in my envelope of cash and he gives me back the change. "You like the picture, Shanny, or are you sending a post card?"

"Both."

"You have a friend on vacation?"

No. Well, kind of. "He's not on vacation," I say. "He's on a journey of the soul." (Really, Mike is the only person who wouldn't think I'm crazy for talking like that.)

"That's great."

"He's in Peru."

"Fantastic."

"Volunteering with kids."

"Wonderful."

"What?" I ask.

"Nothing," he says with an irritating grin. "But you are blushing."

Oh. "I'm just so proud of my art." I say.

"Yeah. I buy that," says stupid Mike. (No I can't call Mike stupid- he's wonderful.) "Anyway, Shanny, here's your post card, for your friend."

"Thanks." (Geeze.)

"And I just have a thought for you to think about."

Hmm… "Okay."

"I think you should take a class. Maybe through a college or an art school? You should take some photography classes. Learn about the machines, about image making, about prints and equipment and techniques and presentation and Photoshop and all that."

That actually sounds great but how would I do that?

"I appreciate the thought Mike," I say. "But I'm strapped for cash. As you know, I don't work for Doug anymore. I need to find a job. This morning's visit was part of my procrastination."

"Hmm." He is thinking. Thinking hard. Oh no. I hope he doesn't think that I'm trying to mooch off of him for a job. I can't bear for people to think that I'm trying to mooch.

"I'm not trying to guilt you into giving me a job," I blurt out.

He looks a little taken aback by my burst of energy. "I didn't think you were, Shanny."

"Oh, good."

"But maybe I can help. I can't give you a full time job, but I could use a hand maybe three of four times a week. If you could watch the shop for me, I would be able to go out on shoots."

"You go out on shoots?"

"I used to. I still get calls but I'm usually so busy here that I can't go."

I really think about what to say. "I think I would love to work here with you, for you, Mike. But I don't know anything."

"It would be a steep learning curve, that's for sure."

"And I'll need to find another job to earn enough money."

"Sure," he says, deep in thought again. "Do you read books Shanny?"

I laugh a little, surprised at the question. "Uh, yes, Mike. I read books."

"Often?"

"I think so. I'm not sure how you define often."

"More than one book a month?"

"Oh- yeah. Maybe two or three a month."

"Stay right here," he says and grabs his hat. (He has one of those old man fishing type hats, only it has no colorful flies on it. How cute is that?)

"Wait. What do I do if someone wants to buy something?"

"Just keep them talking. This is training day number one. Keep them talking, let them look around but don't let them touch things until I come back."

"How long are you going?" I call after him as he heads out the door.

"I don't know," he calls back.

What the heck, Mike?

I don't know what to do so I run through a quick game of 'what if' in my mind. What if I owned the shop and was manning the place? I would stand behind the counter. So, I stand behind the counter. What if there were no customers for a few minutes? I would, argh, what would I do? Dust? Sweep? Admire my work? Straighten things up? That is what I can do. Straighten things up. So, I putter around and tidy things. I wind the straps on the camera bags the way the really neat ones behind the counter are wound. I try to make everything look the way the best items in the store look. I think Mike would like that.

Next I sort the post cards. This shop is so quiet. I wonder if Mike would consider playing music in here. As I try to put the post cards in the most logical order I can devise, the bell rings. Someone is coming in. Ack! What do I do? And she looks fancy. So does he. Dang it! They'll probably want something pricey and fancy that I have no idea about. (Telling them about the nine zone grid will not impress these two, I can tell.) Where is Mike?

"Hi. Can I help you?" I ask. (No, no I cannot help you. Why did I open my big mouth?)

"I think so," says the woman. "We want to take a look at the pigeon picture."

"Pardon? The pigeon picture?"

"Yes. Our friend Bill told us there was a fabulous photograph here. A 16x20 print of a pigeons. We'd like to look at it."

Holy. What?

"It's in the window?"

"Is it?" she asks.

"Yes. I'm not sure if Mike, the owner, would want me to take it out of the window. Sorry. But you can look at it from outside." (Way to promote your own work, Shanny, you goob.)

"Oh yes. I can see it, kind of. Come on Beth. We'll be right back." says the man.

I try not to be some creepy lurker staring at them as they stand in front of the window looking at my work (my work!) But I notice them pointing and laughing. Then they seem really deep in thought, like they're talking quietly as though in a museum. They've probably noticed everything wrong with my work. They're probably too intelligent to want a picture of diseased urban pigeons. They're probably wondering why their friend (was Bill his name?) told them to come down here and waste their time.

I go back to wait by the counter. I don't want to watch them walk away. But then I feel so ridiculous to be just standing there accomplishing nothing. I wonder, would it be totally unprofessional to play Bejeweled on my cell phone while I'm just standing here?

But hold the phone. The couple comes back into the shop.

"Bill was right. We have to have that photograph," says the woman as the man (her husband?) nods enthusiastically. "But we don't see a price tag. Can you tell us how much it is going for? And it is an original, the only print of the image?"

Umm… "I can tell you it is an original. It is the only print but I don't know what Mike is selling it for. Do you mind waiting for him?"

"When will he be back?"

Umm… "Any minute now so far as I know." (It's not lying.)

"Alright then. We can wait for a few minutes," she says. Then the two of them turn their attention to picturing where they are going to put the picture in their house.

This is kind of unreal and I'm trying not to eavesdrop (I swear I'm not trying to be some sort of creepy eavesdropper.) But my curiosity is so electric it's making my fingers itchy. If I don't talk to them I think I may start drumming my itchy fingers aggressively on the counter and that would be loud and unrhythmical no matter how hard I may try to be the opposite. I just need to gird up my loins (although I don't really know if I have any loins) and get the courage to speak.

"So, why did you choose that picture?" I ask.

They didn't hear me. Eugh. Take two.

"What is it about the photo that you like?" I ask.

They turn and look at me. They seem surprised, but hopefully not annoyed, at my question. They sort of chuckle in that grating self-satisfied way. (I know exactly what that sounds like because I do it often enough.)

"We don't like the photo at all," she says.

Oh.

Wait. What?

"But we need it for a gift," he adds.

"Yes. The grotesque nature of the subject will work perfectly for our friends."

Grotesque nature? I don't really know what that means. I mean, I know I think pigeons are gross, but I'm pretty sure gross and grotesque are a little different. But if they don't like it, why do they want to buy it? Maybe they're going to smash it to bits or do something shocking to it at some glamorous grotesque party. (Do such things exist?)

"Well, that's nice," I say because I can think of nothing else. "Mike should be back soon." Suddenly I'm getting my back up. Maybe I don't want these people to buy my 'work.' Maybe my 'work' doesn't belong in their pontsy grotesque-ish apartment.

Not that I can afford to be picky, but it does make me wonder about all those famous long-dead artists that Doug used to go on and on about. He would always talk about how true artists didn't sell out and if they were alive to see how so many rich people, who think they know something about art, pay ridiculous prices for a piece just because of the name attached to it, that those true artists would be sick and destroy their own works just to keep them out of the hands of pretentious pirates. Well I don't think I'm that bad (I'm sure I'm not) but I am starting to get a sense of Doug's righteous indignation.

The thought that I don't even like the pigeon picture pops into my head accompanied by the thought that I do like the money in the envelope in my purse. So, I somewhat easily abandon my high artistic principles. (Maybe Van Gogh would have been as sensible had anyone wanted to purchase his works before he died. Yes. I'm sure good old Vincent would back me up with my pragmatic decision making.)

The doorbell dings again. Oh no. More customers? How did I get into this? Now it's a teenage girl and her mom. Can you say spoiled? It's obvious from the way the two of them stride in wearing the Ed Hardy t-shirts that they think they own the place. Maybe my refusal to serve them will seem like a socio-political statement. (I could slam my hands down on the counter, or point at them and then gesture towards the door as though I am a mute, oh no as though I am a mime. How could I think such a terrible thing? But as I see the girl messing up my carefully wound camera bag straps, I understand again how think such a terrible thing. I've lost my senses.)

"Miss? A little help please?" says the mother with a grating voice.

I am just about to answer her with the same tone when Mike rushes into the store. He swoops around, managing to help everyone quickly and efficiently. In the speed of light, he gets the mother to buy the daughter the (to use her words) "ultimate" camera with so many functions that will never be used but that fetches Mike a decent profit. (I forbear from telling the mom that her daughter hardly needs such a designed machine to take half-naked pictures of herself in a mirror to post on Facebook.)

Next, he focuses on the grotesque couple. I tuck myself into the corner. I really am blushing now as Mike negotiates the price for my print that no one likes. He seems to be taking out any frustration on he may have on his little calculator. (Poor innocent calculator.) After ten agonizing minutes, they leave the shop with the print in tow, looking completely self-satisfied.

Mike waves me over to the counter.

"You're going to have to learn how to deal with all this on your own, Shanny," he says. (Does he have to sound so disapproving? What training did I have? What was I supposed to do?)

"Alright," I say.

"And you're going to have to deposit this cash on your way home," he adds and passes me another wad of cash. Two hundred and thirty-three dollars! "I deducted to the cost of the frame and all that again."

"How much did they pay you?"

He has a sort of wicked grin that makes me glad I'm on his side. "They paid me five hundred dollars for it."

"Five hundred dollars?! Are they crazy? Are you crazy? How did you come up with that number?"

"Well Shanny, really, depending on who came in to buy it, the price may have changed. It was obvious they had the money *(yes it was)* and it was obvious they really wanted it *(yes it was)* but not for any really good reason."

"What's a good reason?"

"It didn't move their souls, Shanny."

Of course. The soul thing again. Mike is right. It was clearly not soul-stirring to them, but how could a photograph of filthy pigeons in a filthy square move someone's soul?

Mike repeats himself kind of. "A work of art should move your soul or it's not the right piece for you. And so any schmuck who wants to buy a work for some less than pure reason deserves to pay through the nose for it."

(I'm reminded yet again why Mike and Doug are friends.)

"Alright. I bow to your philosophy, Sir," I say grandly and (of course) I perform a sweeping bow.

"You should bow to my generosity too."

"Alright, I do."

"I've found you some work, Shanny."

"I know. Here at the shop. That's great."

"Yes. Here. And at my wife's book shop."

Huh? "Pardon?"

"My wife Janine runs Howard's book shop. We've decided. You're going to be on the books working here full time and when I don't need you, you'll work at her shop. And when you start taking classes, we'll work around that. That is if you want the work."

If I want? Geez. I was totally right. This guy is my Yoda or my Richard Geer in "Pretty Woman" (except that I'm no prostitute and he is more like my grandpa- never mind, that was a bad analogy.) I take a quick internal check to see if this is what I want. Yup. It is.

"Thanks, Mike. Thanks so much," I say and shake his hand. I feel a tiny hint of that need-to-sneeze-might-cry feeling.

"Let me be clear that you are not going to become a millionaire working here."

"I never thought I would."

"We're going to pay you thirteen dollars an hour to start out with. We'll see if bonuses can be a factor. And if you keep taking great shots, we'll keep them in the window and see how many of them we can sell. And we'll see if maybe one day someone will really connect with one of them. Now, since your plan for the rest of the day is now irrelevant, let's get to work."

      I just beam. I can tell I'm not blushing. I'm just super thankful. This is great. More than great. I'm going to have to work really hard to live up to what Mike's done for me. How did he get to be so nice? Maybe there's some kind of story there. Maybe there's a reason he's so nice to me. I'll have to tap into my investigative side later. For now, Mike is about to orientate me on the inventory.

Chapter 24

Shanny is... cast-free.

3 people like this.

Muriel Hardy- That's great Shannon. How was Dr. Shoker?

Shanny Hardy- Dr. Shoker is doing well. She said the foot is looking good.

Connor Hardy- So does that mean you are ready for an exercise program?

Shanny Hardy- Connor, I was born ready.

Connor Hardy- Is that sarcasm? Cause I'm serious. Let's get to work!

Oh, Connor. Bless his heart. He's always looking out for me. (That's what I'm choosing to tell myself anyway.) Getting rid of the cast was amazing except for the trauma of seeing the forest that's grown over my lower leg for the past two months. But that was easy enough to fix.

I think maybe now that I can move around easier, I will go back to Italy. I still have money left. (Totally kidding.) I'm not going to make the same mistake. I'm actually only four dollars and thirty-one cents short of my goal. And this afternoon when I get my next pay cheque I will be well over that amount and I'll have enough to start saving for the class I want to take in January. I'm pretty proud of myself. In one month I've managed to earn and save the cash.

Here's how I did it:

1) Working full time at the photo store and book shoppe.

2) I stopped buying ice cream, music off iTunes, and magazines.

3) My insurance settlement money

4) I sold (well, Mike sold) two more of my pictures.

5) I won two of the contests Doug entered my work into. (One was a cash prize. The other prize was a computer program with image editing software. Why would Doug enter that one? Doesn't he know I'm about the bills? Actually, it was pretty nice that he did that for me. I used some of the prize money- and my employee discount- to buy Doug one of the lenses he looked at every time he came in the store.)

I also held myself back from buying a new outfit for my Connor's wedding or for Coen's party which is Tomorrow night.

I did finally text Coen back to let him know that I would be coming, that I was home, that I was fine, that I was still the same happy/non-confrontational Shanny. After that reply, he had very few follow up questions. Only one actually. He wanted to know if I was bringing a date to his party. I thought of all the things I could say (minus the expletives.) I even considered calling Sam Haire (who according to Ryan still likes me) and inviting him to come along. I decided against that. Inviting him to come with me would be the equivalent of buying a piece of art that has no effect on my soul (unless something can make your soul fall asleep.)

It is against the normal philosophy of the perpetually single gal to purposely go to a party alone but I've figured out that I'm hardly normal. (Besides I am planning on walking in, petting Emperor, dropping off my gift, wishing them luck, and running out of there- not exactly activities that require a date.) I have no doubt that all their guests will be fabulously dressed, standing around holding their champagne flutes (why are they called that? Do they play airy music?)

I decided to buy them a Safeway gift card. It wasn't the easiest thing in the world to go in there, but I think it will be worth it. Val may not get the joke, but Coen will. (And besides what else do you buy for someone who has his own house, can buy what he wants, and hates anything knickknacky or sentimental? I was considering giving him the choker he'd admired at Ryan's wedding but I decided against it.)

Unfortunately for Ryan, I suffer from a lack of creativity. I bought the same thing, the Safeway gift card, for her baby shower. (They definitely didn't waste any time starting their family. Or it was an accident. But I don't think Ryan would leave such a thing to chance.) I don't know anything about babies. Her shower isn't for a couple of months but I just thought I would be prepared. I bought the tackiest, corniest card I could find. I know she'll love it.

When I told Mike about my planned gift, he shook his head at me and told me to offer to take some portraits for free- they would still pay for the prints but the session would be free. (After helping Mike work on two photo sessions, I will just say that such a gift is worth way more than one would think.) I thought about it, and decided I will offer that to Ryan. She may not accept, she doesn't know about my new thing. (I'm so excited that I have a thing.) But maybe she will. (Needless to say, I will not be offering the same thing to the happy couple.)

At this moment, I am tidying up the books in the sci-fi fantasy section in Janine's shoppe. Crazy religious people make their way into here stealthily, pretending to peruse the books when really they're jamming their pamphlets into the pages. (On the bright side, if I want to know the truth about just about anything, I have cards with numbers to call and they'll answer all my questions. I do have a question- why not be upfront about it? None of the cards identify which church they're from or which religion. It seems sort of cowardly to me. But it's more than that- it's annoying. Every week, I have to flip through these pages to check for cards and every week there are more- like they're mating. I really hope one day I catch someone in the act. Or I hope one of the weirdos who is in here every day obsessively reading books in the fantasy section- without paying catches them and they have an epic battle. I can picture it: light sabers vs. the bible; magic spells vs. the Battle Hymn of the Republic; Harry Potter's wand vs. Pat Riley's shakes. Who knew battles could be so delicious?)

"Are you still cleaning out those books, Shanny?" Janine asks me.

She is sitting behind the cash counter on her spinny stool, reading Dan Brown's latest thriller, wearing a beautiful pashmina. She's always cold. I learned very quickly not to suggest that the reason she's cold is because she won't turn up the thermostat. (Janine doesn't like being told what to do. There was a younger employee who really got on her nerves doing that- hence, the job opening for me a month ago.) The funny thing is that she doesn't even like Dan Brown's writing, but she reads everything he writes. She feels it is her duty as a book shoppe owner to stay abreast of as many books and authors as she can so that she knows what she's talking about. (It works. She's good at it. She is the one who convinced me that when I'm in the need for a good cry, there's nothing like a good Maeve Binchy story. And when I'm in the need of a good laugh, there's nothing like a good Nick Hornby- though some of the male mentality stuff is reminds me too much of a person I know.)

"Yes. But I have only one row left."

"And then you're off to cash your cheque and solve your mystery."

"Yep."

"Why don't you just go now?" she says and hops down from the stool. She grabs my cheque out of the till and brings it to me.

"Are you sure? I can finish this pretty quick."

"Shanny, the sooner you go, the sooner you'll have your answers and come back and tell me who your mysterious donor is."

"I know who it is, Janine. *(Well, I'm pretty sure, like 90% sure I do.)* That charity company won't tell me who sent the money no matter what. I'm going to meet a rep from the Donor Foundation." They answered my inquiry on Wednesday and called to say that the recipient's family is open to meeting me. Tonight I'm getting the information and signing some release documents or something.

"It is still a mystery because you don't know who the recipient is yet. What do you know other than it's a young boy?"

"Nothing. Except that they live in town." I say over my shoulder as I head into the back room to grab my purse. One of the great things about working here is that there is no uniform. There's practically no dress code except that Janine expects everyone who works here (in other words, herself, her niece Liz, this crazy guy named Wentworth, and me) to dress in a "polished, professional, pleasing" manner. (Whatever that means to us individually.) The store makes pretty good money. Janine and Mike just have some kind of magic touch when it comes to retail. I once suggested she should write a book about owning a small business and she thought I was making some clever joke using her profession as a pun. I was not.

"It's all very exciting," Janine says as she finishes straightening the books. "Are you nervous?"

"I don't know. Kind of. Less than I thought I would be. More than I'd hoped. I think I just want to get it all done. Like it will lift a weight off my shoulders."

"It will, Shanny," Janine says and pats me on the back as I open the door and she turns over the 'Open' sign.

I was surprised that I so easily told Janine and Mike about my predicament but they're like, they're like, well, they're like parents. Like how I wish I was with my parents. I can obviously never have that relationship with my dad and there is just too much (too much something) between me and my mom that keeps us from being close. I guess I just get this sense like Mike and Janine don't judge me. Don't get me wrong- they're both critical enough. They're the first to point out when I say something stupid or wear something ugly or make a mistake. (They also have acid tongues when they find a creative work that doesn't live up to their standards.) But when it comes to important things, they are the proverbial wind beneath my wings- not in a cheesy way.

"Wish me luck," I say and smile.

"No worries there," she says and adds, "You're working tomorrow morning with Mike at the shoot?"

"Yep. I'll be at the zoo at five a.m. Looking forward to it."

"Good. I'll let him know. I'll have him bring you breakfast."

"Thanks."

"And I'll tell him not to ask you any questions because I want to hear about it first."

"Well, I'll have more to tell on Saturday. I'm hoping to meet them tomorrow night, then go to that awful party-"

"Aww, Shanny-"

"I know. But maybe it won't be so bad because I will have had a really good experience and I'll be on such a high that I won't care who's in love with whom." (Being around Janine has improved my grammar too.)

"I hope so."

"I'll see you Saturday, Janine."

"Bye, Shanny."

I hurry off to my car, so happy to feel the lightness of not having a cast anymore. I stop at the bank and deposit my cheque in the drive thru window-teller-machine-thing. (Lazy, I know, but the air conditioning makes staying in the car mighty tempting.) Next, I make my way over to the local chapter of the National Bone Marrow Foundation (Dr. Shoker gave me the address after she took off my cast.) The drive is not that far but, as usual, I take a few wrong turns and end up at the wrong location. (I definitely need to consider asking for a GPS for my Christmas present. I'm sure if Liam knew all the mistakes I make with my pathetic orienteering, he would buy me one tomorrow.) Finally, after making so many goofs, I end up at the office.

The receptionist is pretty friendly and tells me it will be just a short wait. I can't imagine they're really that busy, but what do I know?

I am summoned into the office.

What the?

How is this possible?

Catherine Sterling is sitting in the cheapo desk chair. Have I stepped through some kind of portal? Am I accidentally at the insurance office?

"I recognize you," she says.

Yeah. I'm the girl who stopped her brother from punching you with a stapler.

"I remember you too. I was in your insurance office just over a month ago I think."

"Right."

"You made me feel like I was a big liar." (Argh. Shanny, don't be so blunt.)

"Well, I think we do that sometimes. It's part of the job requirement. When you interview for the post they ask if you know how to hurt peoples' feelings."

"They must have hired you on the spot." (Shut up!)

Her eyes flash with a wild sort of anger, but quickly calm down. (I knew I took it too far.)

"What can we do for you today?" she asks snidely.

"I called about connecting with the recipient."

"Oh, yes."

Her words are oh, yes; her tone is oh, no.

"I was told that they were happy to meet with me."

"Hmm," she says as she looks through a stack of papers. (How many papers could they possibly have filed on this? Can't she just give me the information?)

"I was told that tomorrow would be the time we'd meet."

"Hmm." She is lucky Liam is not here. But I might have a violent outburst.

"Is there a problem? Do you need to see some I.D. or something? I was told-"

"What you're told over the phone and what you're told in person sometimes vary."

"Should I come back?"

"No. I didn't say that."

You're not saying anything. You're just playing solitaire with you sheets of paper you power-tripping volunteer.

She stands up and asks if I will excuse her for a minute. I nod of course and she leaves the room. Aha! She left the stack of papers on the desk. (I refuse to say her papers or her desk. She doesn't own any of these things.) Oh man. I've got to know what it says. Is there a problem? Is there some form that shows they gave me the money and she is going to try and extort that money from me?

I try to stealthily lean over the desk and look through the papers without touching anything. (Think Catherine Zeta-Jones in that old Sean Connery movie- stealthy like that.) But I'm too busy worrying about my posture to actually be able to read anything so I run around to the other side of the desk and- Ow! I bang me knee on the corner of the desk and I reach down to grab my knee (because what else do you do when you bang something?) and- Ow! I hit my head on the corner of the desk. Ow. Ow. Okay. I get it. I give up. I go back to my chair.

Catherine (Sterling, not Zeta-Jones) comes back into the room and promptly sits in her chair. She officially shuffles her sheets into one big pile and looks up at me.

"What happened to your face?" she asks me bluntly.

Huh?

"Your face? You're bleeding. What happened?"

I'm bleeding? I reach up and touch my forehead. Eugh. I am bleeding. I must have cut myself when I hit my head. Darn it.

"Why are you bleeding, Ms. Hardy?" she asks impatiently.

Umm...

"It just happens sometimes. When my head hurts."

That was maybe the stupidest thing I've ever said.

She is just shaking her head at me, but at least she passes me the form with the contact information. Before I grab it, I ask if I can use one of the tissues on the desk (not her desk.) I just take a couple, ball them up, and hold them against my head. With my other hand I grab the form.

Catherine still looks overwhelmed by my weirdness but my shenanigans have apparently encouraged her to speed this along.

"The meeting is planned to be tomorrow night at the Tim Horton's on 5th and Main tomorrow night at six-thirty. Does that still work for you?"

"Yes." (I get meeting at Timmy Hoho's- it's in public but not stuffy; you can eat or drink without it being a long meal where you're waiting for service, etc.; and it's not in their home which may feel too personal.) Six-thirty makes sense too. It's after dinner but it's not too late. For me, six-thirty makes things a little complicated. Should I wear my party outfit to the meeting? Or should I get changed in my car? (I will not change in the bathroom at the Tim Horton's.) Maybe I'll pull a half and half sort of thing. Like I'll wear my top and earrings and all that but change into my skirt later.

"Well, good. Good bye, Ms. Hardy."

Ack. How long have I been sitting here thinking about this? Time to get off your butt and head home, Shanny.

"Good bye, Ms. Sterling."

With my hand pressed against my forehead I try to rise with as much dignity as possible and walk out of the office. Ow. My elbow hit's the door frame. Maybe I shouldn't drive home? I'll just sit in my car and wait for a while.

I am excited. I can't deny that. I just can't wait to see them and give back the money that they gave to me. It's going to be great.

Chapter 25

Shanny Hardy commented on Ryan Cooper-Kokozka's picture, "the bump."

Shanny- Ryan, you can't even tell you're pregnant. You're tiny.

Ryan Cooper-Kokozka- Do you mean you don't believe me?

Shanny- I'm giving you a compliment!

Ryan Cooper-Kokozka- Haha. Thanks Shanny.

It is the moment of truth. I hope I don't look too dolled up for our meeting. I had to have a nice long shower to get the smell of the zoo out of my hair. This morning was hilarious- unintentionally hilarious- and laborious, and smelly. But, as expected, Mike did a great job. I could tell just from seeing the images uploaded onto the computer that he got images they wanted for their new campaign. (I really had no idea what a reputation he had when I met him. And for some reason he's taken me under his wing. Bless him. And Janine.) I'm sure the zoo will be overjoyed with the images. We took a little longer than we'd expected but any time spent outdoors, taking photographs, learning from Mike is a great use of time in my book.

So, I got home, filled out the cheque, leaving the 'to' line blank. (I'm not sure which member of the Lorenz family I should be presenting it to. I'm sure they'll let me know.) Then I had my marathon shower, blow dried my hair, tried to curl it, gave up, straight ironed it. I put on enough makeup to look decent but not desperate. And I will wear… eenie, meenie, mynie, mo- the blue silk shirt. (It's actually my favorite. The ruffles are great but it has a loose thread. I snagged it on a nail once. Long story.) This shirt looks great with my fake Majorca pearls and a simple black pencil skirt. So, that is what I'm going to wear. For now, I'm wearing it with a pair of jeans and my black heels. It will be easy enough to swap the skirt for the pants.

And now I am off to the Canadian corporate Mecca of coffee, doughnuts, and soup. (It is strange that our country's pervasive culinary delights are sandwiches, baked goods, soup, and hot drinks. Hot drinks that you can order without feeling stupid- unlike some places I could name.) This place at least I know how to find. I drive with my skirt hanging from the rear passenger window (who needs to shoulder check anyway?)

And here I am.

Deep breath, Shanny, deep breath. Here it goes.

I walk in the restaurant. I'm trying to smile and look oh-so-casual. How am I supposed to recognize them? I should have thought of that before.

The restaurant isn't very busy for early on a Friday night. Usually it's full or people grabbing a coffee or a muffin or something before they go to the movies. I look through the place. I'm not here for the two old couples sitting in the booth in the corner (what are they-on date night?) I'm not here to meet with the group of teenagers sprawled over three tables as though they are having a study group when it is hardly the first week of school. The only other option is a blonde woman; she looks like a mom, sitting alone with a mug. But can that be her? I thought I would be meeting the family-not just the mom. I'm not sure what to do.

I kind of subtly-ish walk towards her. Nothing happens. So, I circle around as though I need a better look at the menu or the available baked goods. I can't just stand here. So, I take another lap, fighting the temptation to look at my cell phone and pretend I have a text message or something.

I stop in front of the mom-looking lady (mom's definitely have a look don't they? And I don't mean tired. I mean something kind of intangible, something that, as a PSG, I do not have, something that I kind of want.) Be brave, Shanny. You can do it.

I try to look as non-weird as possible in case I'm wrong. "Excuse me," I say. "Are you waiting for someone?"

"Shannon Hardy?" she asks.

Oh good. Good job, Shanny. I am a good detective after all.

"Yes, I'm Shanny."

"I'm Tessa, Theresa, Lorenzo."

"Nice to meet you."

"Nice to meet you. Um, sit down."

"Great. Thanks." I can't quite pinpoint the feeling here; it's not awkward, but it sure isn't comfortable.

She picks up the conversation right away. "How are you feeling? How was the surgery and the recovery?" (See, she is such a mom.)

"I'm doing good," I say. "Recovering from the transplant part was the easy bit. The only hard stuff was the injuries from the accident."

"I'm sure, yeah. You looked a little banged up."

Aha! I knew it! She snuck into my room and dropped of the cheque. Otherwise how else would she know that I looked like a mess? (Well, I guess someone could make assumptions but they wouldn't say that I looked banged up. Would they?)

I'm going to call her out and get to the point.

"I thought you came into my room."

"Oh." She looks really surprised. "I was sure you were asleep."

"You came in and gave me something."

She nods.

"Money?"

She looks surprised and opens her mouth to say something but then abruptly closes it as though she's not sure if she should defend herself or accuse me of something. The wheels are turning in her brain- I can see them.

"That was actually why I wanted to meet with you, Tessa. Oh! Not because I want money. No, no, no, no, no. *(Have I ever said no so fast?)* I wanted to meet you because I wanted to return the money," I say and I reach into my purse to grab the cheque.

"You want to return the money?"

"Yes. If you can just tell me what name to put on the cheque, I'll fill it in right now."

"But why do you want to return the money?" She looks really confused. Like I've lost my mind or something. Like I'm speaking Esperanto again.

"I've just felt funny, no, that's not it. I feel wrong to take it and I really need to give it back. Please don't be offended. I really appreciate the thought, I do. I just need to return it."

"Sam wanted you to have it."

"Sam?"

"My son. He insisted that I go home and bring him his piggy bank. It wasn't really a piggy bank. It was a Sydney Crosby coin bank- that's what it was officially called. He bought it after the Olympics. Sydney Crosby was all he could talk about."

I smile. (This kid wasn't the only one who was obsessed with Sid the Kid after that overtime goal.) But I don't understand, how does a young boy have fifteen thousand- Oh- Shanny, you are so stupid.

"Two quarters and a twenty dollar bill," I say.

"That's right," she says. "It was all he'd managed to save but he insisted that I hurry home and get it for you. And then he pulled a rose out of a bouquet someone had brought to him. He said I had to take that too. He wrote the thank you note himself. On a scrap piece of paper and he got his dad to bring him an envelope. We didn't have any. Anthony went to the shop and bought a whole box of envelopes just so that Sam could have one. He insisted on sealing it up and everything."

"I had to bite the corner to open it."

She laughs at this. "What?"

"My hands were bandaged, I couldn't rip it on my own and I was curious and impatient, so I ripped it with my teeth."

"Sam would have liked to see that."

"I can add the twenty dollars and fifty cents to the rest of the total if you like."

"What do you mean the rest of the total?"

"The other money you gave me."

"That was it."

What? Have I got this all wrong?

Tessa keeps explaining. "We didn't have anything to give you. We weren't even sure if we were allowed to give you his envelope, but Sam kept pestering Dr. Shoker about who the donor was and eventually she told him that you were in the hospital. She told me where your room was once I had the flower and the envelope. She thought it would be alright for me to drop it off as long as I didn't disturb you." She sounds apologetic. She's getting upset. (This is not how I wanted things to go. What is happening?)

"You didn't disturb me. I was just confused about something. I'm really sorry to make you upset. I'm sorry. I just wanted to meet you and make something right."

"You tried. I know you did. We all wanted to thank you. That's why I came. But Anthony just couldn't. He just felt it would be too hard."

"It would be too hard to meet me?"

"It's just that it's still feels so, like it just happened."

She is not talking about surgery. I cannot ask this question. I cannot ask what I think she is saying. And this cannot be. I refuse to believe this.

But there she is- sitting in the Tim Horton's- crying. She's trying not to, but she is crying. What do I do here? I can't do anything. I can't go back in time and make my bone marrow the magic cure it was supposed to be. All I can do is apologize.

"I'm very sorry Tessa. I'm so sorry. I'll go."

She grabs my hand just as I get up and try to leave. "I'm sorry. I didn't plan to tell you. I feel just terrible."

I've got to get out of here. I can't breathe.

"Please don't apologize. I hope everything will get better. Good bye," I say. Because what else could I possibly say?

I hurry out of the Tim Horton's but at least I have enough composure not to run in my heels. I get to the car and climb into the front seat. I grab onto the wheel and my knuckles are almost turning white from my grip. I am not doing this again. I am not going to cry in a parking lot. Again. Come on, Shanny. I start the car and look in my rear view mirror to make sure it's safe to back up. I see my skirt hanging in the back. Coen's party.

I drive way faster than I should and I roll the windows down. Maybe if I have some air I'll be able to breathe. What was she saying? That he insisted se give me one of his flowers? I didn't even take it home. It didn't smell good. I just left it on the food tray. Why did I do that? Come on, Shanny. Why didn't you keep it?

Somehow I end up at Coen's. I have to park far away because the street is lined with cars. I don't even bother changing into my skirt. I can't stop myself. I'm practically running to the door. I'm not carrying anything but my keys. My bag (and so Coen's gift) is still in the car. For a street with such little traffic, there seem to be way too many cars in my way. Go ahead and honk. I don't care.

I end up at Coen's door pounding on it. I keep pounding. I can hear how loud it is inside-that people are laughing, that music is playing. Maybe they can't hear my knock. But I don't care. I'm not going in there. I pound on the door. My knuckles start to hurt. I hear someone inside call to Coen and tell him to come and get the door.

The door opens. It's him. He has a martini glass in his hand and he's wearing a new suit and a new tie. (At least they're new from the last time that we were together.)

"Shanny?"

"I just came to tell you that you were right. You were right."

I turn and rush down the driveway, clumsy in my heels and jeans.

He calls after me, "What are you talking about Shanny?"

"You were right okay? You know better than me. I'm just stupid."

He's almost caught up to me. "Shanny, what's going on?"

"Just what I said," I yell in his face. "You were right. I shouldn't have done it. It was a waste of time and I was stupid to think I was helping someone."

When did the ground get so shaky?

"Shanny?"

"He's dead!" I cry. "Okay? He's dead." The grass is wet. I can feel my knees getting drenched and I can't calm down. Am I the one making that sobbing noise? I can't think about that now. This isn't far. This is all so stupid. Nothing about this is right.

Coen is down, kneeling next to me, trying to hold onto my shoulders. "Who's dead, Shanny?"

"Sam."

"Sam Haire?"

"No! Not him. Sam! You were right. I didn't save anyone's life. He gave me a flower and his money and then he died and his mother just stared at me and tried to apologize when it's my fault and she shouldn't have bothered coming to meet me because what I did didn't help."

"The boy with cancer?" asks Coen quietly. "He didn't survive."

I can't even answer. I just shake and the tears pour out of me as though they can't bear to live inside such a weakling. They have to get out of me- they have to escape as fast as they can. I can't fight them back so I'm just going to let them.

"Shanny, why don't you come inside?" he says but then looking towards the house, he changes his suggestion. "Why don't we go for a walk?"

"No," I say and I get up. "Go back to your party. You can tell them all how smart you are and how your stupid friend is completely clueless."

"Come on, Shanny," he says and reaches to grab my arm but I jerk it out of the way before he can. "Come on. Let me take you for a walk." (What is he, the dog whisperer? And I'm some sort of unbalanced problem dog?)

"Go inside. They're waiting for you," I gesture towards the house. Of course the door is open and people are there- watching us.

"Hey guys, I'll be in in a minute," he calls over his shoulder.

"You're going to miss my toast," someone calls. Who is that? "Oh. Hi Shanny," says the voice. It's Grant. One of our mutual friends. Great. "You come in too," he says. "It's going to be a wicked good toast. I'm not too drunk yet."

"Just go inside guys. We'll be in soon," says Coen. "Come on, Shanny. You got dressed up and everything. Come inside. We'll cheer you up."

I get up and stare Coen in the face. "No. Going in there will not cheer me up. Nothing about this situation will cheer me up. I didn't come here to be cheered up. "

"Then why did you come here? To be a total bring down? You go away. You ignore my calls. You hardly answer my texts. And now you show up at my party just to yell at me and have an emotional breakdown over something that was not even within your control. This isn't you, Shanny."

"What is me?"

He doesn't answer. He just looks confused, like I've gone crazy.

"If I'm none of those things, what am I? You know everything, right? So, what am I?"

"You're a mess," he says and tries to smile in his charming way, as if that will make me feel better. In fact, it does the opposite.

"Good bye, Coen. Have fun at your party."

I get to the end of the driveway. He's still following me.

"Shanny, you didn't even know the kid. I get that you're sad but keep some perspective."

Is that what I am, the girl without perspective?

I keep walking.

"Shanny, where are you going? You shouldn't drive when you're this upset. Stay here tonight. I can end the party early. You can stay with me and Val."

"What would make you think I want that? Go inside. Leave me alone."

"Leave you alone? You're the one who came here!"

"I know. Because I thought you could make me feel better. Of everyone in my life, you're the one who usually does. But that's all changed."

"Because I'm engaged?" he asks bitterly.

"Because we can't be close anymore. That's all over."

"What are you really saying, Shanny?"

Stop crying already. "I'm saying congratulations. Good bye." I pull my shoes off and I run to my car just managing to dodge one last truck that pulled out blindly from the nearest driveway. The honking drowns out whatever Coen yells at me (and whatever the driver might be yelling too.)

My car seems to have a mind of its own and it takes me to Mom's house. Why would I come here? I never tell her what's upsetting me and she would hardly be sympathetic. But maybe there's some good food inside. That always cheers me up. Standard single gal protocol- replace physical affection and emotional reassurance with food. Yeah, she must have something in there.

I'm about to pull into the driveway until I notice two cars are already taking it up. (Thank goodness someone invented headlights or I may have hit them.) I recognize Liam's car but this other monstrosity is completely foreign to me. Who's here?

I walk up to the front window where I see lights on. Like some poor orphan kid in a depressing Christmas movie, I stare in at the happy family enjoying their robust meal. In this case, Liam, Kim, Mom, and Chance Barley are all sitting at the table eating some sort of pasta. (I can see the long drippy noodle- fettuccini maybe? - from here.) The food looks delicious. There's nothing like a good bowlful of carbs to ease any level of heartbreak. But I decide to play the martyr and sneak away. But just then, my mom looks out the window and sees me.

I hear a muffled "Shannon?" through the glass and sheepishly nod. I must look completely crazy. My jeans are grass stained,

my face is runny mascara stained. I can't
imagine what my hair looks like. And my shirt is
probably ruined. And my friendship with Coen
is probably ruined.

My mom and the others look completely
baffled. She tries to wave me in but I don't want
to go in. Liam gets up, says something to
everyone else and comes outside. He grabs my
hand and drags me to sit next to him on the front
steps.

"If you want to, you can talk to me," he
says and just sits there next to me, perfectly
willing to wait until I have something to say or
not.

We sit for a few minutes. The early
September wind rustles through the trees. We
can hear it more than we can see it. It is pretty
dark after all. Then something inside of me just
breaks and I tell Liam everything. I tell him that
Coen and I aren't friends anymore, that I bought
and wrote Charlie a postcard but didn't know
where to send it, that I worked so hard to earn
the money to pay back the cheque but it was all
for nothing, and I tell him that Sam is dead.

Liam doesn't say anything. He just
exhales, making a kind of whistley sound. He
hooks his arm around me for a strong side hug. I
start crying again, but this time it's not violent
sobs. Liam just stays next to me. He doesn't give

me advice or anything (how un-brotherly of him.) But he does say something that surprises me.

"You know, Shanny, you really wear your heart on your sleeve. You don't think you do, but it's there- and anyone who bothers to look can see it."

Is that true? I hope that's not true. That's the last thing I want.

He goes on, "And anyone who sees it, knows how good your heart is."

Huh.

"Do you have the postcard with you?"

I nod. "It's in my purse."

"Why don't you give it to me? I won't read it. I'll try to get it to Charlie."

I have him the postcard. "Thanks."

"You're welcome," he says and puts the post card in his fat wallet.

Kim quietly comes out and silently offers us lemon squares. Liam takes two. Kim takes one and sits on Liam's other side. I take one too. The three of us sit there, just eating our lemon bars. It's nice for almost half an hour.

Then Mom comes out with Chance.

"I can't take being in the dark anymore," Mom says. "What is happening, Shannon?"

"It's just been a pretty bad day," I say, trying not to sound overdramatic.

"She's had a rough day," Liam agrees. "I don't think she wants to talk about it."

"Oh Liam, she'll tell me," says Mom. "Shannon, what did you do?" (Of course that's what she asks. The only reason I would ever be upset is if I did something…)

I have to say something. She won't let me out of here if I stay silent. But what am I supposed to say with Chance Barley standing there? (And is he Mom's boyfriend? Is it official? Eugh.)

I decide to tell them one thing. I try not to get too riled up.

"I went to see the family of the boy who got the transplant with my bone marrow."

"You did?"

"Yes."

"And it didn't go well?"

"No. The boy wasn't there. He didn't make it very long after the surgery. He died."

"Oh. Oh, Shannon. I'm sorry," Mom says benevolently. (Am I supposed to say thank you?)

"Thanks, Mom," I say.

It's quiet again for a few minutes.

"But Shannon," says Mom, "why did you go to meet them? Is that okay? Is that normal?" (What a weird question.)

"It's not abnormal."

Chance is evidently curious too. He looks on as Mom asks again, "Why did you meet with them? Did they want to meet you?"

"I just wanted to meet with them."

"Your mother asked you why, Shanny. That's not an answer," says Chance.

In unison, Liam, Kim, and I look up at him.

"Did they want to meet with you?" he repeats on Mom's behalf.

I stand up. "I think I'm going to go home now. Thanks for the lemon square. Good night everyone." I walk down a few steps, but, as seems to be the pattern tonight, someone calls after me to stop me.

"Shannon, your behavior is very rude."

"Mom," Liam softly interjects.

"Don't make excuses for her Liam. I know she's had a difficult day but that is no excuse to be so rude, refusing to answer me and now ignoring Chance."

"I'm not trying to ignore anyone," I say.

"I'm sure you're not trying," says Mom. "You're naturally good at it."

Liam shakes his head and Kim is trying not to watch.

"Not in the mood for a lecture, Mom. Give me a break."

"You shouldn't speak to your mother like that Shanny, no matter how upset you are."

"I'm sorry, Mr. Barley, but no one asked for your opinion. Who are you to tell me that?"

"Shannon!" My mother is shocked at my rudeness but I have no more sensitivity; my nerves are just frayed. I've lost my sense of having done a good deed, I've lost my best friend. I don't care about losing Chance Barley's good opinion.

"I'm going home." (Maybe I should get a t-shirt that says that. Or 'good bye.' I've said that a ton lately too.)

"You should show some gratitude Shannon," Mom says. "You owe Mr. Barley that at least."

"Muriel, it's alright. Don't press the issue," he says to my mom.

Now, of course, I can't just storm off to the car. "What are you talking about, I owe him?"

"You wouldn't have had your little Italian escape if it hadn't been for his generosity," Mom says proudly.

His generosity- what is she talking about?

"Yes, I know about the cheque you received, Shannon. The one for fifteen thousand dollars. You didn't think that money came out of nowhere?"

Oh no. How can this be? I look at Chance and my mom in a mix of disbelief and disappointment.

"That's right," Mom says almost triumphantly like she's defeated me in some way. "Chance arranged for that cheque."

"It was you?" I ask incredulously.

With a show of false modesty (that is so easy to recognize), he nods and looks down.

"Why?"

He looks at Mom. Oh man. This is unbearable. I'm part of some chivalrous show of male power in an attempt to impress my mother.

"Well, that's good," I say. "Now I know who to pay back." I pull out my cheque and write in Chance's name. I pass him the cheque. "Thanks, but no thanks," I say. "I don't want the money."

He takes it but says, "I am not going to cash this, Shanny."

"Please do. I don't want the money."

"Why not?"

"That's my business. I want to give the money back."

"Well, as I've said, I will not cash this cheque."

"I don't want it," I insist as Chance rips up my cheque.

Liam intervenes in this merry-go-round of an argument. "Shanny, he's not going to take it. You can just donate it to someone or some organization if you don't want it."

(What a reasonable suggestion.) "Fine, that's what I'll do then."

"That is not why I gave you the money," says Chance sounding pretty edgy.

"Well, I'm going to do what I want with it if you won't take it back," I say. "And that means I am going to get rid of it as soon as possible."

"Really, Shannon," says Mom, "you embarrass me."

"Then I really better go now. We wouldn't want that," I say.

For the last time that day, I get in my car and drive. This time I wind up back at my apartment and all I wish is that either I could 'Eternal Sunshine' my memory or that at least I had a dog to keep me company and listen to me complain all night. Instead, the only thing I have to keep me company is a big pillow and a bucket of rocky road ice cream. (I have a year's ration of that stuff stored in my freezer.) What an overwhelming day. I will be happy not to have a day like this again. Ever. I change into my pajamas and I try to turn off my brain so that I can sleep. I can't quiet everything but maybe I can at least focus on something semi-positive.

The thought circles through my head- who am I going to give this money to? It has to mean something and go to someone who deserves it. Maybe this won't be so bad after all.

Chapter 26

Shanny is... confused.

I'm also at work now. Janine's sympathy is overwhelming. I hope Mike comes by and asks to take me over to the photo store. I would like to be away from weirdo Wentworth and the incessant empathy. Mike's Yoda-like wisdom may come in handy. His occasional silence may as well.

Instead of enjoying the photo store, I am using a hair dryer to melt glue and remove old discount price stickers. (I know- my talents are innumerable and impressive.) I'm not unhappy here but this was not the premise on which I accepted work. I'm more than not-happy, I'm still and positive. The sound of the hair dryer drowns out Wentworth's humming at least. (I only wish I'd had it earlier this morning when he spent twenty minutes arguing with two teen girls about Twilight. Wentworth insisted that they should be neither on team Edward, nor on team Jacob, but that Bella needed some time to become her own person.)

Anyway, next Tuesday is Connor and Meaghan's wedding. (I know- who gets married on a Tuesday?) Being the sister of the groom is pretty much a non-job, much less demanding than being Ryan's bridesmaid. (But really, performing brain surgery on a helicopter would have been less demanding than being Ryan's bridesmaid.) All I have to do is show up and be ready to take two or three standard family photos. No problem. All I need to do tonight, or any night before then, is iron my white blouse and black skirt. (Not so that I will look like a waitress; their colors are black and white.)

I'm impatiently waiting for my lunch break. Lucy is bringing lunch. We're going to eat at one of the picnic tables on the promenade in front of the shop. In the summer you can never find a seat but now that it's September, people have this automatic it-must-be-getting-cold reaction and the benches are generally free. It's a perfect day for outside lunch- it's 24 degrees and little bit cloudy. Perfect weather.

I have about one more hour to wait. I fill the time in several ways:

1) I finish removing the stickers.

2) I have an argument with Wentworth about his assertion that the Bronte sisters had an influence on Franz Kafka.

3) Janine gives me three hugs and two pats on the back.

4) I help an older gentleman find a copy of every WWII book we have in the store.

Overall, it's a fine morning and when Lucy arrives I am hungry and ready for whatever she brought me.

We're parked at the bench, eating such a fabulous fruit salad and spicy chicken wraps.

"This is great, Luce," I say.

"Thanks, Shanny. I'm so glad you called. I miss working with you. But this place seems more fun, more you."

Yet another person with their statement about what I seem to be.

"Well, I had two reasons to call you," I say. "I definitely wanted to see you. But I wanted to give you this, too."

I pass her an envelope and tell her that she can open it now or she can open it later.

"Are you kidding?" she says as she tears into the envelope. "Hang on, Shanny. Why is there money in here?"

I smile broadly. "I'm going to explain as concisely as I can. Someone gave me money and I decided to do something good with it. That money is for you to give to the Special Olympics or to help your church group do something good or anything you can think of to make the world a better place."

"Really, Shanny?"

"Really, Luce."

"Ahh!" She leaps up from the table and gives me a big hug just as I'm about to stick a fork full of fruit in my mouth. (Fortunately, accident averted.) "You are the best, Shanny! The money will be put to good use. I promise!"

"I know you'll do something great with it."

We chat like old friends, catch up on everything. I really like this kid. She's the way I want to be. Maybe I am a little bit like her. I hope so, anyway. We finish our lunch and Lucy heads to Safeway to start her Saturday afternoon shift. I have this real sense of contentment. I don't think I could have given five thousand dollars to anyone more deserving. Another five is going to the SPCA (I hope there's a way that I can tell them to spend the money on dogs. I'm sorry, but I just don't care about cats- they're mean and frightening. They hiss!) I have a plan for the other five thousand but it requires a little more maneuvering before I know for sure if it'll work.

I get up from the table and promptly bump into Wentworth. Was he standing there the whole time?

"What are you doing?" I ask.

"Did you give that girl money?" he asks.

(He really does not have social skills. Why did Janine ever hire him?)

I'm so taken aback that I answer him. "Yes," I say.

"Why?"

"Because it was a good thing to do."

"It might be a good thing to do to give me some money."

"It might be, but I'm not going to," How he manages to look so sadly surprised is beyond me. Did he really think I would give him money? What a nutbar. (Why are nuts grouped in with being unbalanced or crazy? What did they ever do to anyone? Well I guess a lot of people are severely allergic to them…)

"Come on, Wentworth, let's go back to work."

"That's why I came out here. They want you over at the photo store. I was going to bring your bag but I thought that might be an invasion of privacy."

(But eavesdropping isn't?)

"Alright. Thanks."

I hustle into the store and grab my bag. After another hug from Janine I manage to extricate myself and walk the block down to Mike's store. (I think it's great that the two stores are a fair distance from each other and that they never tried to do something crazy like merge them into one shop to save the money on rent.)

The store is Saturday busy (in other words there are about four customers.) I dash behind the counter and drop off my bag then take over till duty for Mike so that he can consult with a grizzly bearded man. My guess is the man wants to do some serious nature photography. (He's got to capture that Sasquatch, he's just got to!)

Within a half an hour, Mike and I have taken care of the customers and there is a bit of a lull.

"So, that's why you needed my here Mike?" I ask. "Do you want me to go back to the book store and just wait for you to page me over? (Wait a minute- that sounds a little too much like Safeway style. Not good.)

"I did need your help, Shanny. You can stay here now. Janine called. She told me what happened."

"All of it?"

"Yeah. She doesn't keep much to herself."

"Well, she wouldn't keep things from you."

"She used to. *(Really?)* We had to work on that. When we first got married, she kept a lot of things in. We both did I guess. But we got used to each other, to telling each other everything. And now here we are and-"

"And you can't get her to stop talking?"

(I'm so glad he knows that I'm completely kidding.)

"Sometimes." He smiles. "But what I'm wondering is if you have someone to talk to about all this stuff you have going on. I think you need to have that, Shanny."

"Well, everybody needs that."

"Yes."

"Not everyone gets it."

"Maybe not. But you deserve it. So, I want to know why some young man phoned me this morning to find out when you would be working here."

Who did what now?

"I don't know."

Who was it? It must have been Liam. No one else knows. Could it be Charlie by any chance? (Eugh. Poor choice of words.) Maybe it's Charlie.

"He's going to be here any minute now."

As if on cue, the doorbell chimes and we turn to see who it is.

It's the grizzly man again. I'm pretty sure he's not my gentleman caller.

Mike lifts his eyebrows at me- double time- and I have to try really hard not to laugh. Apparently the man wanted to start taking pictures with his new telephoto lens right away (I mean right away- he just walked to the edge of the parking lot and started playing with his camera. Creepy…) But he couldn't get the lens cap off. I don't quite accept that Mike didn't show him how to before, but Mike kindly refrains from rolling his eyes and shows him again. And again. I can't watch anymore. It's too painful.

I grab the Windex and Mike's specially purchased window cleaning cloths (no streaks!)

Hoping that the physical exertion will clear my mind (as well as the windows) I attack the front door and the front windows with vigor. I'm just about finished, just wiping up the bottom of the window when I hear a tap from the outside and I see a familiar pair of stupidly expensive shoes.

I try to stand up without hitting anything (no such luck) and leave the bottle and cloth on the floor. Then I remember how important the front display is for Mike's shop. I scramble to grab it all and carry it to the box where it must be stowed (upon penalty of death.)

Conrad still hasn't come in. So he wants me to go out there? What is this- manipulation? Well, I'm not playing that game. I'm done. I'm finished. I'm- surprised he's coming in.

Mike is trying to watch me as he's helping the parking lot peeping tom who is packing his things up. I'm not really sure what I'm supposed to say or feel right here. I wasn't expecting him to be here and now that he is, I realize that it's not anything that I wanted. I can tell this is just going to be drama. (And I, like Mary J., want no more drama.)

I decide to play stupid.

"Can I help you?" I say in my polite retail worker voice.

He's not having any of it. "Yeah. You can tell me what the hell that was last night?"

"I can't actually. I'm working."

"Fine," he says and grabs an SD card from the rack on the counter. "I'll buy that."

"Your camera is a Sony. They don't take SD cards," I say.

He just stares at me.

"It's your money," I say and scan the disk. I tell him the price.

He pulls out his wallet, closes it, and then says, "I've changed my mind. I don't want to buy that."

Mike has made his way over. "Is there a problem here?"

Suddenly, charming Conrad makes an appearance. "No. Mike, right? There's no problem. I just want to talk to Shanny. About yesterday. I spoke to you on the phone earlier."

"Right," he says, his eyes still on me. "Do you want a minute, Shanny, to talk to him?"

I force a smile. "Sure."

"Alright then, head outside for a few minutes. A few minutes."

"Okay."

I follow Coen out of the store and it's so sunny out that I wish I had sunglasses. (That would also cut down on the awkward eye contact.)

I talk first, "How did you find out I work here?"

"That's not what I came to talk to you about," he says sort of surprised by my deflecting question.

"I didn't tell you. I want to know how you knew. Then we can talk about your issues."

"My issues? What's happened to you Shanny? When did you become such a-"

"A what?"

He stops and doesn't finish his sentence. (He is wise.)

"Imagine my surprise," he says, "last night, as Val and I are opening our gifts and I get something with your name on it."

Huh? I don't follow.

"Beth and Karl bought us a one-of-a-kind print to put up in our bedroom. They thought it would be perfect for us. Val loved it. She said something about the grotesque nature of it *(Oh man! What?!)* I didn't particularly care for it. But imagine my surprise when I look in the corner and see your name on it. Was that some kind of sick joke or something? Why would you arrange for them to give us such a sick picture? What is wrong with you?"

He looks so mad but I don't care. Wrong with me? Shut up!

"I didn't arrange for anyone to give you that picture," I say angrily. "They bought it. They came to the store and asked for it. I didn't know they knew you. And if I knew it was for you maybe I wouldn't have let Mike sell it to them. I would never think that piece would speak to your soul-"

"Speak to my soul? Shanny, who are you?"

"So what then? Do you want to return it? You want a refund or something? I don't see it. You haven't brought it with you?"

"That's not why-"

"You can't be mad at me because you have idiot friends who think they're better than everyone else." Wow. My pulse is racing. Have I become moody or what? Maybe I am becoming an artist.

He lowers his voice to try and calm the situation, I think. "I'm not mad about the painting. I was just confused. You cleared it up. It's just quite a coincidence, if you think about it."

"Fine. What are you mad about then?"

"Why did you just take off last night?" he asks and stands closer to me, leans his hand against the lamp post and then takes it off when he realizes the metal is hot even in September. I try to calm down and remind myself that he has been my friend through a lot: through my decision to leave school, through boring days, through being fired from Safeway. He does deserve some sort of explanation.

"I was upset obviously. I shouldn't have come. I'm sorry that I ruined that part of your night."

"Shanny, I was so worried about you. That's why I'm mad. You were acting so crazy. I've seen you upset before but never like that and, and I think there's more to it than you let on."

Tears are gathering to form an assault. I can feel them accumulating.

He keeps talking, "You don't want me to marry Val, do you?"

"I didn't." (Did I honestly just say that? Oh man.)

"And why not?"

I can't look at him. "A lot of reasons." Why is he moving closer to me? What is he doing putting his hand on my shoulder? Knock it off, Conrad.

"I didn't know, Shanny," he says. And then he leans in, too close to my face to talk. Conrad kisses me. The thing, the 'IT' that I've been waiting for and imagining for eight years happens. And his lips taste as good as I'd imagined (not better) and his hands are on my shoulders (not on the sides of my face like I'd hoped) and I don't feel what I thought. His kiss didn't feel like more. That's what I always imagined- that when he pulled back I wouldn't be able, or at least I wouldn't want, to stop kissing him. But that's not what this felt like. It was nice, but it wasn't more.

He whispers my name and kisses me again. He stops. Maybe he realized I wasn't kissing him back the way he'd expected.

"What are you doing, Coen?" I ask. "You're engaged."

"I don't have to be. I love Val. I do. But that could be over. Maybe it ran its course. And come on, it's you, Shanny. I've never gotten along with anyone else the way we do. It's funny, I never thought about wanting you. I just thought you were my friend." He sort of shakes his head and laughs as he looks me over. "You are really good at hiding your feelings, you know. If it wasn't for last night... but now so many things make sense."

The way he's looking at me is driving me crazy. I'm split in two. He couldn't see my feelings until the worst night of my life. And now for some reason he wants me.

"I just- I don't understand. This is too much," I say.

"It is a lot. You're right."

"I don't think I want to risk our friendship."

"We wouldn't be risking it," he says. "We're just going to see where things go."

"Conrad," I say after a pause to catch my breath. "Why do you want to do this? Why take such a risk?"

"Why not?"

"Why not? I can think of about a million reasons."

The first look of worry passes over his perfect face. He's wearing my favorite cologne- he knows it.

"But you love me, Shanny."

"I do," I say but I know I sound unhappy.

"And you want me," he says with his hand under my chin.

I do. I did. I don't know.

"I think that what I want has changed a lot. I've changed a lot in the past few months. I want different things now. I don't even just mean you. So many things about me are-"

He steps back. "Have I just made a complete idiot of myself? You changed your mind or something since last night? You make a total display of yourself and now you've changed your mind. Is that it?"

Please tell me this is a nightmare. Like I am only dreaming that I'm trapped in some heart-breaking old melodrama. Pinch me. Or at least have the decency to knock me out if I'm not dreaming.

Words pour out of me. "You came here. I didn't ask you to change anything. I didn't really tell you anything last night. I was crazy upset and yes, I was in love with you for a long time, maybe since we've met even. But I've watched you with other people before and I never said anything. Even when you started dating Ryan, I never said anything about my feelings. I guess I just snapped last night and I was hurt and sad and maybe it was my messed up way of trying to find closure in all this."

"Well, I hope you've found closure. I have."

He turns to walk away. He must be humiliated. I don't think he's used to being rejected. Is that what I just did? I never thought I would do that.

"I'm sorry, Conrad. When you're not mad anymore, I hope you call me." (Eugh. What a pathetic thing to say.)

"Don't count on it," he calls back.

"You can't just throw our friendship away because of this!"

"Why not?" he yells back without even looking towards me. His car beeps, the unlocking sound. I stand there and watch him drive away. I don't really believe this is the end of our friendship. I hope it isn't. And I'm genuinely sorry that he's embarrassed, that his pride's been hurt. But that's all I feel-sorry. I don't think he loved me. He was just getting that trapped animal feeling and maybe I was his opportunity out of the cage. Maybe he was curious. I know I've been curious about him. I think that curiosity, the unknown, is sometimes what makes people attractive. (And if they happen to be gorgeous and smell good, it doesn't hurt.)

This whole thing was just wrong. Nothing unfolded the way I would fantasize about. But as I think this, I realize that I haven't fantasized about Coen in a long time. Maybe I reached my lusting-after-him expiration date. Maybe I got brain damage when I got hit by that car. Or maybe those feelings got jogged loose and slowly made their way out of my system. Not just to be replaced by my feelings for another guy, but my feelings about myself, about what I want in the world, about who I want to be.

Okay- time to stop, Shanny. You are drowning in the deep edge of the pool. You are not a philosopher. Go back inside. Wash your face. Help Mike for the rest of the day.

I head into the shop and see Mike's concerned but non-intrusive expression.

"I'm okay," I say.

"Never thought you weren't," he replies.

He waits a minute then asks, "That's not the guy you wanted to send the postcard to, is it?"

"No."

"Good," Mike says matter-of-factly as he keeps quietly working away at editing yesterday's animal pictures.

"What happened to the postcard guy?" he asks after another silence.

"Nothing. He's still away I think. No one seems to know when he'll be back, if he'll be back."

"He'll be back," Mike says knowingly.

I hope he's right.

Chapter 27

Shanny is... attending Connor and Meaghan's wedding.

Muriel Hardy- Be on time Shannon.

Ryan Cooper-Kokozka- Tell them congrat.

Shanny Hardy- You're not coming Ryan?

Ryan Cooper-Kokozka- No. I wish. But I'm so exhausted. Pregnancy is exhausting. You'll find out soon enough.

Muriel Hardy- What??? Shannon???

Ryan Cooper-Kokozka- I just meant that someday Shanny will know the feeling.

Muriel Hardy- So Shannon's not pregnant?

Shanny Hardy- Mom couldn't you have called me about this?

Muriel Hardy- I have to go on Facebook to find out anything. You never call. By the way, I am getting married. To Chance. On Christmas Day.

Ryan Cooper-Kokozka- Congratulations Muriel. That's wonderful!

That's my life alright. So many people moving on. And I'm moving along too. Just not in the same ways. My job is great. I'm saving money. I've given away ten thousand dollars of some jerk's money. (Maybe that's not fair.

Maybe Chance Barley's not a jerk. But maybe I don't care to think otherwise just yet.) Moving on- I'm planning to start school in January. I've already applied to two schools. Mike keeps assuring me that I'll get in. It's funny, I was never nervous when I applied for university but now that it's something non-academic, I'm strangely worried.

I try not to think about last weekend. It was just so nuts (sorry pecans) that I want to forget about it. On Sunday night I skipped family dinner. I doubt many of us were there anyway. Connor's really busy with wedding stuff obviously and he's hauling Gavin, his best man, around to everything with him. I don't think Liam went either. He was pretty miffed after Saturday night. But he has to be careful- his firm does a lot of work with Chance Barley's company after all. Who knows? Maybe that was the magical night when Chance proposed to my mother. (I feel strange that my mother is getting married before me. Kind of sick, too.)

Monday was supposed to be a day off but I went into work at the book shop anyway. Janine was fine with me being there. She let me curl up in the red velvet easy chair in her office and she gave me a book to read. No Maeve Binchy this time, she knows I'm too emotional for one of those. Instead, she thought I may enjoy a little non-fiction and insists I read a few chapters of the latest "Freakonomics" book. I'm fine with that. A little critical thinking about social phenomena never hurt anyone (at least that I know of.) I enjoyed spending the day with a book and a fruit smoothie from the Juice Barn next door. (Who named it the Juice Barn? Juice doesn't come from cows. At least I hope not.)

This morning, I've been working with Mike, who's given me tons of tips (too many tips) on wedding photography. I keep reminding him that I'm not taking pictures tonight but he insists that I should take my camera and practice. I wonder if he's planning on letting me work at one of his upcoming bookings. Or maybe I could eventually get hired on my own. Who knows? (Then all the torture of being at a wedding would pay off. Literally. I would get paid. Maybe I should really think about this.)

After lunch, he sends me home and tells me to have a great night.

I get home, take a nap, get dressed, and eat something hearty. (The dinner at the wedding is going to be a vegetarian meal so who knows what will be edible. Whatever happened to prime rib and chicken?) After I finish my food, I grab my camera and get myself off to the botanical garden for the wedding

The ceremony was nice- not really memorable, but nice. (Maybe that's good for a wedding. Usually the memorable moments are created when things that go wrong- drunken uncles, sketchy speeches, fashion disasters, dancing to a Roxette song, those type of things.) Now we're in the conservatory (chichi sounding, isn't it?) There's no head table or guest book or anything like that. (Connor and Meaghan would die before doing anything so traditional.) And they don't have a cake! Like my wish came true. Instead of cake, they have vegan strawberry cupcakes. (I didn't even know such things existed but I am ready to try them out. There is no chocolate though. Meaghan really let me down.)

The emcee announces that it's time for all us to take out seats. I grab Kim a glass of punch and meet her at our table where I'm seated next to Liam and an empty seat. Conrad's name is on the place card. I'd forgotten that he was supposed to be my date. Good thing he didn't show up. There is no way he would after what happened. It still surprises me that I'm not more upset about him. What happened to my heart? Anyway, now I am stuck here at the table with an empty seat to my left as a glaring notification to anyone who looks over that I am here by myself. To top it off, there must be some sort of aphrodisiac in the drinks because everyone at our table is behaving way too affectionately. (PDA's = terrible to the PSG. Especially when the PDA is between your mom and her boyfriend- strike that- fiancé.)

The program is mercifully short. The toasts are bearable. The highlight is definitely when Gavin mentions that for one entire summer in high school Connor ate McDonald's for dinner every night. (If I blush the same way as my brother, no wonder people can always tell.) But then Gavin waxes poetically on Connor as an example of change and commitment and that without a doubt Connor will be so committed to Meaghan. Connor actually cries as he gives Gavin the ultimate bro-hug.

Finally, the parade of speeches comes to an end when Meaghan's grandpa sings her a song in Finnish. It is time to dance.

The lights dim, the sound comes up, and everyone's having a great time. I try to dance and feel the excitement. I feel obliged to take advantage of my freedom from the cast but I'm just not feeling it- you know, the groove and all that. I give up and head to the cupcake table. It's deserted. (This does not bode well for the organic vegan cupcakes.) But I bite the bullet and shove one in my mouth.

This thing is dry. And gross. And somehow turns into a strange paste. Why did I put the whole thing in my mouth? Oh, Shanny, you silly goob. Oh well, at least I'm not trying to impress anyone here.

"Hey, Shanny, do you want to dance?"

It's my younger brother in his grown up man suit (no tuxes for this wedding.)

"No thanks, Gavin," I say but I think what is heard is actually something more like "whogwhagwagin." It's not my fault I'm inarticulate though- I mean my mouth is full of gluten-free gloop. (I really hope they didn't pay much money for this stuff.)

Gavin grabs me a glass of lemon water. I drink it, eternally grateful. But I take so long that Gavin gets commandeered to return to the dance floor. (I think by his girlfriend but I've never met her and I don't even remember her name, so I'm not sure.) As my gaze follows them, I see Mom and Chance slow dancing. While "Footloose" is being played. Why are they so weird?

"Pretty weird, huh?" asks Liam as he reaches for a cupcake.

"No!" I yell as I smack his hand away. Unfortunately, I smack a little too hard and my hand ends up in a pile of cupcakes. I try to subtly toss them into the nearby trash can. "I mean yes, Liam. Mom over there- that's weird. I meant- No! Don't eat the cupcakes. They are terrible. Go get some more carrot sticks or cucumber water or lemon water if you need something."

I look at my brother. He is watching Mom. He looks really disturbed by all this. I pat his back, trying to be comforting. "Maybe it won't last." He looks at me doubtfully. I go on, "Maybe they'll move somewhere hot? Like old people who retire in Florida."

"They're not going to move." He sighs. "Chance told me this morning that since he's going to be my stepfather, he thinks his company should use another real estate firm. So, he's not going to renew his contract with my firm. He doesn't want to appear unfair. He said he hates nepotism."

"What? But you are really good at your job."

"I know." (Liam has no false modesty.)

"Do you think he's trying to send a message after last Saturday night? Is he going to fire Kim, too?"

Liam shrugged.

I go on, "And what's he talking about, he hates nepotism? Charlie works for him and he's his nephew."

"Charlie did work for him. Chance fired him."

Oh no. Please don't let it be because he went to Peru. Please don't let my 'inspiration' be the reason he lost his job.

"Chance didn't appreciate Charlie being out of touch and out of the country for two weeks longer than they had agreed."

Oh no.

Liam continues, "And you know, Chance really hates nepotism. He could hardly let us go and keep Charlie on."

"Did Chance tell you that this morning? You went in to meet with him and he just started firing everyone or something?"

"No, Chance didn't tell me about Charlie," he gestures forward towards our table. "He did."

What?

"Who?" I look over to where Liam pointed and I see him.

It's Charlie. Hey! It's Charlie!

What the heck is he doing here? And why does he look like that? He's wearing a grey suit but it doesn't fit him and he's wearing sandals. He is super tanned. He doesn't look too happy standing with his uncle (I can guess why) who is introducing him to his fiancé. But Charlie smiles politely and shakes my mom's hand.

Liam elbows me playfully. (Was I gawking? I was probably gawking.)

"Go talk to him, Shanny," he says. (Why is Liam forever telling me what to do?)

I don't know if I want to- I do kind of look like a waitress. Why is he here? But as I'm staring his way, trying really hard not to gawk, he looks over. Our eyes meet and his big goofy smile (combined with his hair and his jaw line and his eyes and- oh I'm gawking again) pulls me toward him like he's a fridge and I'm a magnet. (Nah, I don't like that analogy- he is not fridge-like- cold, or side, or boxy, or smelly without baking soda. He's something much better.)

Like I'm in some John Hughes movie, the perfect song starts to play and everyone starts to disappear as we approach each other. I can feel the blush and I just want to laugh- not because anything is funny. This isn't funny- this is wonderful and strange. We meet up somewhere between table eight and table fourteen. My heart is racing.

"Charlie, what are you doing here?"

"I came to see you."

"But here, at my brother's wedding?"

"Liam invited me. This morning. He gave me an invitation. He said you might need a date."

"Really?" (I can't be mad at Liam right now, though I am trying not to feel sooo embarrassed.)

Charlie nods. "You look really nice, Shanny."

"I think I look like a waitress. Maybe I should bring you a drink."

I wait for him to make some remark that builds off my disparaging wit but he doesn't. He just stares at me. He looks so happy and sure of himself in the most inviting way. Who made him this way?

I can't handle the silence. "When did you get back?" I ask.

"Two days ago."

Oh.

"I needed time to decompress."

Oh. I get that. "I totally get that," I say.

"You do, don't you?"

"Absolutely I do."

He laughs a little and nods. (He gets my unconscious 'Office' reference! Oh bless him. Could he be any more adorable?)

"Do you feel like dancing, Shanny?"

Absolutely I do.

"Sure."

He takes my hand but instead of to the dance floor, he leads me outside. There's no terrace or anything but we're on the lawn and we can hear the music.

"I like your shoes," I say as we start to move. "Very formal."

"I can't bring myself to wear dress shoes. It's too soon."

"But you could wear a dress suit?"

"I had to. I didn't think they would let me in otherwise."

"Well, you look nice," I say as I pick a little piece of lint off his shoulder.

His arms are around my waist. I feel like I'm at an awkward school dance or something and he's the boy. He is the boy. He's not my friend. He's something else. And I feel like something else being here with him.

"Charlie, why do you like me?" (I can't believe I just asked that.) "I mean, you do like me, right? Why?"

"I like you for lots of reasons," he says.

"But how can that be? You hardly know me. We've only met a few times."

"What do you mean I hardly I know you. Shanny, I know you."

"No. You know recovering-from-accident-did-something-good-before-she-had-a-breakdown-and-escaped-to-Italy Shanny. And that's not really me, I don't think."

"I don't buy that," he says. "I know you. I'll prove it. Here. You have a good heart and terrible taste in music. You can make a joke out of anything and you risked a lot to help someone you didn't even know."

"I didn't risk much," I say weakly.

"Yes, you did. You risked your heart. I know what happened to that little boy. When Liam told me my heart sunk. I wish I'd been here for you, Shanny. The first thing I thought was how much I wanted to give you a hug," he says and squeezes me tighter in a pure way that makes his intentions completely clear- that it's about making me feel better and not feeling me up. "And I wished I could say something to tell you not to give up being who you are, or something corny like that."

"It's not that corny," I say. It's a little clumsy maybe but the intention isn't corny.

"Well, let me ask you something, Shanny," he says as he gently spins me out and spins me back in to him. "You like me."

"Yes." Was that the question?

"Well, same deal. You hardly know me. Why would you like me?"

I wonder is this the kind of honest conversation Mike was talking about.

And I wonder how Charlie could even ask me this?

"I'll give you a list if you like. It's not the full list, but it's a start. You bought me a lemon tree because you think I like plants; you fed my friend's dog when I was in the hospital; you have terrible taste in music; you think I'm funny; you sent me a postcard- not an email or a text- a real postcard; and you make me feel like I'm a good person. *(Oh no- tears approaching.)* You make me want to be that good person; and when you smile, Charlie... Do I need to go on?"

He's looking at me so seriously, like I'm saying things he'd never heard but like he understands them. (Not like I'm speaking Esperanto.)

"You don't need to go on, Shanny," he says.

"But so, you see, when we stack things up, there are like a million reasons for me to like you. Not so many for you to like me."

"Are you really this insecure?" he asks.

"I don't know. I never thought I was insecure. Maybe I am a little bit." The song changes but we keep dancing. This song is even slower. I've never heard it before. It's so beautiful. "I think maybe I'm just nervous. I don't have a very good track record with this kind of thing. Actually, that's not true. I don't have any track record." (How's that for honest?)

"Sometimes no record is better than a bad one. It's like a clean slate."

That was actually a really nice way of putting it. I just rest my head against his chest and shoulder as we dance slowly, swaying side to side.

"You know why I came tonight?" he asks.

"Because you kind of like me."

"I more than kind of like you, Shanny. But that's not the only reason I came. You know what happened to me this morning? I got fired. I got fired by my own uncle. And I didn't even care because three minutes earlier I got a postcard."

A postcard? I don't interrupt. I just let him keep talking.

"I got a postcard with a picture of a bridge on it. And one of the lines said, and I quote, 'I dreamt the other night that you were drafted into the Peruvian soccer league. I cried because you didn't come home. Isn't that ridiculous?' I read that and I decided, I've got to see this girl right away."

"Liam gave you my postcard? I tried so hard to figure out where to send it while-"

"Meanwhile there I was, in my South American hovel thinking you didn't care about me. Even after I told you that you were my inspiration. And I came home and there was no note or anything."

"I didn't forget you. I read your postcard every day. I even took it with me to Italy." (Oh no was that T.M.I.? Am I completely pathetic?)

He kisses me on the cheek. "You are so different from any girl I've dated." (How he manages to say that without it sounding derogatory in any way is a mystery to me. A beautiful mystery.)

"I'm going to think that's a good thing," I say.

"It's a very good thing. It means the odds are in our favor. At least until Chance and your mom get married and we become stepcousins."

What? "Charlie! That is not a pleasant thought."

"Them being married or us being distantly related?"

Eugh. Either. Both. I can tell he's totally kidding, but still. I look closely at this handsome man in a suit and sandals.

"You know, you're kind of weird, Charlie."

"So I've been told."

I realize something and I'm so excited. "That's it- you're a weirdo!"

"I am?" he asks apologetically.

"Yes! You are a weirdo, a perfect weirdo." I can feel my smile spread so far it almost touches my ears. He is too. I quickly file through all the things he's done and said. Buying me a lemon tree? Taking pictures of Coen's dog? Taking off for three months and getting fired? Coming to a stranger's wedding to tell me he likes me? He's wonderful and he's weird. And maybe he's mine.

"Sorry."

"No. Don't apologize, Charlie. It's wonderful. That's why, that's why-" I interrupt myself, surprising both of us, I kiss him. I full on kiss him. And he holds me so tight and kisses me back.

And it feels like more.

We just keep dancing out in the wet grass. The music changes and we keep dancing- until the chicken dance plays. Then we walk through the lit part of the gardens, catching each other up on our separate adventures.

"Would you go back?" I ask him.

"To Peru? Yes, I think I would."

"Would you go somewhere else on a good will humanitarian-type trip?"

"If I had the money I would."

"What if I had the money?" I ask him and proceed to fill him in on my big plans, my crazy hopes. I know this is all a crazy risk but nothing about me is normal. That's what all the nonsense of life lately has unveiled to me.

I tell him about all the websites I've searched, all the possibilities for doing something for people that they can't do for themselves. He seems excited but he has some reservations.

"Are you sure you want to do that, Shanny? You're sure you want me to come?"

"I am. We'll have to go soon. I'll be starting school in a few months."

"I never expected such an offer. I never thought you would be a sugar mama."

I laugh. "I'm not. I'm just trying to be a good person and I need to bring my inspiration with me."

"And you're sure you want to spend your money this way?"

"I can't think of a possible way to spend the money any better."

"Will you want me to pay you back?"

"No. You can pay for the next trip."

"The next one, eh?" he says as he laces his fingers through mine.

"Oh yeah. This is going to be an annual occurrence. Even one day if there are babies around, we'll drag them along with us. *(Argh. Shanny stop yourself!)* Not to say that there will be babies- I just mean-" I sigh lamely.

Charlie laughs at me.

"No explanation required you crazy girl. We'll cross that bridge if we get to it," he says and squeezes my hand a little tighter. "But for this trip. Well, just remember you've never gone on a trip like this before. You might hate it. You might need recovery time."

"I'm not going to be a princess," I say. "When we go, I'll be hard core. Then, when we come back, I'll be normal Shanny and get ready for school."

"When we come back, I'll be a bum," he says. "I'll have to start a major job search."

"You'll have no trouble finding a job, Charlie. Just think of all the good karma you must have."

"I'll have to get my neighbor to keep Karma for the trip. Hopefully, he won't mind extending his stay."

What is he talking about?

"Who's Karma?" I ask.

"My dog. He's a complete mutt, but he's my best friend. The only way I can leave is because I know my neighbor is taking good care of him."

This guy is too perfect- for me. I can feel his hand holding mine but that's not enough proof that he's real. I fling my arms over his shoulders and look up at his face willing him to kiss me. It doesn't take long. And it's even better than before. And it still feels like more.

Chapter 28

Shanny is… off. She's going to be a good person- with a little inspiration.

Connor Hardy and Lucy Adams like this.

Muriel Hardy- What are you on about Shannon??

Ryan Cooper-Kokozka- Did you take off again? Stop doing that.

Muriel Hardy- What! Where did she go this time??

Gavin Hardy- She's in Honduras.

Muriel Hardy- What is she doing there???

Gavin Hardy- What she said, being a good person.

Muriel Hardy- I don't understand why she can't be a good person at home?!

Janine and Mike Austen- Shanny is a good person at home. You have a great trip Shanny! Take lots of pictures. Send us a postcard!

Shanny Hardy- Be back soon! Talk to you all when we get back.

…the end

H.E. Rae is the pen name of Elisa McRae who once attempted to roller blade. She also wrote "The Perpetually Single Gal"- not an autobiography- and the sequel, "The Currently unSingle Gal."

To fund her excessive lifestyle of eating French cheese and taking her dog for walks to the park, she works as a high school teacher in a small city outside of Vancouver, BC. She loves the rain, ironic sitcoms, and spending time with her family. She has read "Pride and Prejudice" thirty-seven times and the last "Harry Potter" book once.

Under the name E.M. McRae (her actual initials) she has written a trilogy of YA adventure books called "The Order."

Ebook versions of her books are available from iTunes.

You can follow her on Twitter @Elisa_McRae or on her sporadic blog at elisamcrae@blog.ca .